Who hasn't thought Pride and Prejudice could use more dragons?

Praise for Maria Grace

"This lady does know how to tell a story and how to invent an incredible new world ." **From Pemerley to Milton**

"Maria Grace did a wonderful job spinning a tale that's enjoyable for Austen lovers who do and who don't typically delve into the fantasy genre because she does a great job balancing the dragon world she has created alongside Austen's characters." **Just Jane 1813**

"It's a brilliant world Maria Grace has dreamed up and researched meticulously... based on dragon lore of Britain, Scotland, Ireland, and northern Europe.." **Medative Meanderings**

"I was ... surprised by how well this concept worked. Maria Grace makes the introduction of dragons into Regency life seem seamless, ... It's by turns clandestine and tense, and playfully silly, and I found myself weirdly invested." **The Boot Rat**

A PROPER INTRODUCTION TO DRAGONS

Maria Grace

White Soup Press

Published by: White Soup Press

A Proper Introduction to Dragons
Copyright © 2018 Maria Grace

For information, address
author.MariaGrace@gmail.com

ISBN-13: **978-0-9980937-8-9**
(White Soup Press)

Author's Website: RandomBitsofFaascination.com
Email address: Author.MariaGrace@gmail.com

Dedication

For my husband and sons.
You have always believed in me.

1
Chapter

April 1801

The front door creaked open.

"Jane! Lizzy!" Mama shrieked, her skirts swishing and shoes scuffing as she walked. At least it was a happy sounding shriek, not the one she used when she was displeased.

Elizabeth looked up from her sewing just as Mama appeared in the parlor doorway. Perhaps it was just as well. The seam on Papa's shirt was nearly mended, and she rather dreaded the fancy work that Mama would have her do next.

From the look of the packages Mama carried, she had been to Meryton this morning. Odd, it was not the usual day for her to go. Unexpected shopping trips often made Papa unhappy. Hopefully this one would not leave him too discomposed.

Jane set aside her sewing and rose as Mama trundled toward them, muttering under her breath about the sun in the room. By late afternoon, the parlor tended to become uncomfortably hot, but near midday, as it was now, it managed to be quite comfortable. Some might consider the room a bit shabby, with sun-faded furniture and carpeting that had seen several generations of Bennets' footfalls. Elizabeth found it welcoming and cozy with large white peonies on the paper hangings and happy yellow curtains that fluttered in the light breeze. She stabbed her needle into the seam she was stitching and stood.

"Was your trip this morning pleasant?" Jane's voice and expression were so sweet it would be easy to think her disingenuous.

But no, if there was a single word to describe her eldest sister, it was sweet. Unfortunately, it proved a mixed blessing at best. On the one hand, it was a very pleasant thing to have a sister who was so kind, but on the other, it made comparisons awfully difficult. Mama was very apt to draw them between her two oldest daughters.

Mama dropped down on her favorite chair and plopped a package wrapped in brown paper on the nearby table. She dabbed her forehead with her handkerchief as she caught her breath. "Come, come, girls. I have something special that I want you to see."

It was some consolation that the package was the wrong size and shape to be yet another bundle of ribbons and lace. While those things were often pretty, they were hardly worth such a fuss.

Mama untied the package as Jane and Elizabeth drew straight-backed wooden chairs near the table.

"I ordered these for you last month, and they have

finally arrived." The brown paper fell away to reveal two books, one bound in green and the other red, each about an inch thick, with nothing on the cover or binding to reveal what was within.

Mama had bought them books? Why? She felt reading was hardly a good investment of a young woman's time.

Mama handed the green one to Jane and the red to Elizabeth. "You have both been working very hard on your writing. Jane, your hand is quite lovely now. Lizzy … ah, yours has definitely improved."

"Thank you, Mama," she muttered under her breath. It was true that Jane's penmanship was beautiful and that hers would never match that standard. That still did not make it pleasing to hear it voiced. It was not as if Elizabeth's was difficult to read. She just did not favor the romantical curls and flourishes that found their way onto Jane's pages, but Mama thought those elegant and therefore better.

"You both are big enough now that you ought to begin keeping your own commonplace books." Mama clasped her hands before her chest and beamed.

Jane smiled as well, but was it because she should or because she was genuinely pleased? One could never be quite sure.

"I have kept one since I was your age. By now of course, I have a number of volumes. They have been ever so helpful to me. One can never seem to remember just the right turn of a phrase for a letter or recall which book she read it in when she needs it. But, if it is in your commonplace book, then you will always know where to look. The same is true for bits of wisdom you read or hear, a special receipt you might be given. I even wrote the instructions to make the breeches ball that finally cleaned those odd stains off your father's buckskin breeches. Sister Phillips sketches in hers at times to remember room designs or garden plans. You can place any number of important things you might want to remember there."

Jane ran her fingers across the edge of the pages. "It is very lovely, Mama. Thank you."

"Yes, thank you." Elizabeth clasped the book to her chest. "I am most excited to begin! I can think of a number of things I have recently read that I would very much like to write down."

"Excellent, I am very glad to hear that. It will be lovely for you to have a reason to practice your writing without being reminded to do so." Mama smiled as though that were a genuine compliment. Perhaps she thought it was.

But it did not really feel like one.

"That is all well and good." Papa shuffled into the room, slightly bent over, his feet dragging just the barest bit over the carpet.

Earlier this morning, he had been complaining about his joints aching and demanded a cup of willow bark tea from Mrs. Hill. He had been doing so more often recently, three mornings during the last week. Had Mama noticed?

"Mr. Bennet! See what I have bought for the girls."

Papa took the book from Elizabeth's hands and riffled through the blank pages. "Very good, very good. See that you write sensible things in there, Lizzy." He raised his bushy eyebrows at her, a peculiar look in his eye.

Elizabeth blinked several times and pressed her fingertips to her lips. Well, that was not among the things Mama listed as appropriate for a commonplace book, but certainly, if she was to remember important things, then the things she studied with Papa should definitely be written there.

"Lizzy will need to come back to this later. For now, I need her to accompany me." He handed Elizabeth a small notebook and pencil. "I need her to write notes for me as I examine some of the land."

Mama harrumphed. "I suppose she may go, but it is all so very peculiar. Why should she be writing for you? Since you insist you cannot do it yourself, you ought to have a secretary."

"And yet you insist on the need for lace and new gowns. Which would you prefer to have?" His eyes narrowed and tightened at the edges, lips pressed hard together.

"Such a curmudgeon. Go with your father, now, but do not forget to make your hand neat and proper as you write for him." Mama waved them out of the room.

Mrs. Hill handed Elizabeth her bonnet as they headed for the front door. Papa said nothing, his jaw tense and teeth clenched tight. That he was quiet was hardly unusual. Mama did most of the talking for them both. But it was difficult being reminded that writing hurt his hands, something Mama did not appear to grasp.

A soft, warm breeze greeted them as they left the house, tickling her cheeks as it passed. What a perfect April day, warm enough that one did not need a spencer but cool enough that one did not find herself in a continual state of inelegance, as Mama was wont to refer to it.

Papa remained silent as they followed the path through the gardens and into the woods.

"Where are we going? I thought you said we were going to check on the fields," she asked softly, so he could ignore the question easily if it irritated him.

"I implied it, but never actually said so. I wish to take you to a place you have never been before. One that is at the heart and soul of this estate." His lips turned up at the corners, just a mite, but it was enough to break her tension.

"Do you mean—"

"Yes, I want to show you where Longbourn lives."

"Will I get to meet him?" She clutched her hands into fists to contain the glee that threatened to burst forth.

"No, not yet. You are not ready. But this is the first step in preparing you to meet him."

She swallowed back a huff. It would not do to be too open about her disappointment. "I do not understand. For what must I prepare? I know what he is. I have seen drawings of his kind. I have read all the descriptions. What more must I do?"

His forehead creased just a bit. "My dear, it sounds so much simpler in the lore than it is in real life. I have met grown men who fainted dead away the first time they were introduced to a major dragon."

Was he laughing at her? Elizabeth harrumphed. "But I will not do such a thing. You said it was quite remarkable that I could meet Rustle when I was only four years old and think nothing of it."

"Rustle is a cockatrice and not a particularly impressive one at that." Papa scratched the back of his head. Though he was friendly with Rustle, he never had been especially impressed. "He has been a faithful friend of the Gardiner family for almost fifty years now and is most sympathetic to the concerns of the family."

"Since Rustle is a friendly dragon, my meeting him—"

"Was important and remarkable to be certain, but it is not the same as a major dragon. You must trust that I know what I am doing. I am taking you to his lair today so you might see how large a creature he actually is, and that you might become accustomed to the peculiar odor dragons have."

"The dragon musk the lore talks about?"

"Some find it quite offensive." Papa rolled his eyes.

"I am sure I will not." She crossed her arms over her chest and straightened her back. She would not be persuaded otherwise.

"Of course, child, of course." Papa may as well have patted her on the head, considering the tone he used. "Now remember, if Mama or your sisters ask, we have been to the fields that flood in the spring. You cannot talk about this jaunt with any of them."

It was rather fun to have a special secret to share with Papa, but sometimes it was so hard not to talk about something so wonderful with someone else. Especially Jane.

The woods became darker, filled with old hardwoods, their branches arching overhead like a sort of woven roof over the pathway.

"These are the sort of woods that dragons like. Many old shady trees with limestone underground—it is called a karst terrain—that makes many caves and crannies for them to use. And see there," he pointed toward a clearing, "look closely, and you will see the entrance to Longbourn's lair."

Elizabeth crouched and peered at the hillside at the far edge of the clearing. Hanging branches obscured the opening, but when she stared at it, she could just make it out. It was a little taller than the cellar ceilings, which she was told were tall compared to other houses, and about half again as wide. If Longbourn did not duck to go inside, he could not be more than fifteen feet tall. For a dragon, that was not so very big.

"Impressive, no?" Papa nudged her with his elbow.

She chewed her knuckle. "I suppose. It is not as large as I had thought. Must he fold his wings to enter, or is it large enough to accommodate his wingspan?"

He seemed a little disappointed at her question. Perhaps he had expected a greater level of awe in her reactions. "Wyverns generally do not walk about with their wings spread. They only do so when agitated or ready to fly."

An odd earthy, musky scent wafted toward them on the breeze. Dragon musk. Rich and loamy with just a hint of ammonia and rot. She wrinkled her nose just a mite. It was not so much unpleasant as it was unfamiliar.

He waved her up to stand. "Come along, that is enough for now. You have seen where he lives and can recognize his scent. That is good. What do you think?"

Entirely anticlimactic was not the answer he was probably looking for.

"Since your mother has given you that book to write in, I think it would be good for you to write what you have seen today and your impressions of it. It seems a thing worth remembering." Papa put his hands on his hips and arched back just a bit. Walking even short distances was becoming more difficult.

"But will Mama not want to look at what I have written in my book? You have said many times that she cannot hear dragons so I must never speak to her about them."

"Ah well, I am sure it will come as no surprise to you that your mother is most unlikely to give much thought to your book again now that she has given it to you. It is not in her nature to follow up on things. Once they are begun, they are generally forgotten. In the odd case that she thinks to ask, I trust you will be able to readily distract her from it." He shrugged. "Hurry up now. Since we are all the way out here, there is something else I should show you."

They walked a little farther to the place where the woods bordered the fields.

"There is a harem of fairy dragons that live in these woods." He pointed up into the trees. "They prefer the sunnier parts of the woods, nesting high in these trees. It is a little late in the day now to hear them, but if you come out earlier and listen carefully, you may be able to hear them, possibly even see some of them. Be careful though, as their songs are very soothing and can even make you sleep."

Elizabeth giggled. It seemed a fitting means for the tiniest of dragon species to protect themselves.

"And there," Papa pointed to an odd creature jumping after something in the fields, "that is a tatzelwurm."

She clapped her hands over her mouth to contain a squeal. She would get to see a dragon today after all!

"He is an old tatzelwurm called Rumblkins. He was hatched in the barn and has imprinted upon men, but does not choose to keep their company. Like his kind, he is a bit grumpy and unsociable."

She crouched, hands on her knees, to get a better look. "From the front he looks like a very large tabby cat."

"Indeed he does. His front feet look like cat paws as well, but they have thumb-toes that set them apart from actual cats. That is how you can always tell a tatzelwurm."

"Does not their back half look like a snake?"

"It does if you have not been persuaded away from seeing it. They are some of the most persuasive of dragons. That is why they are often seen living among people, passing themselves off as cats. Most of the best ratters and mousers are actually tatzelwurms."

She snickered. The idea of people welcoming dragons into their houses unbeknownst was rather charming.

"Look at the way they move—see how he coils his tail and springs forward, a spring-hop as it were. Some say it addles their brains and makes them all very stupid."

"What an unkind thing to say!"

"You may find it very accurate when you finally get to know one."

"When might that be, Papa?"

He sighed, rubbing the back of his hand along his jaw. "I cannot tell you. Tatzelwurms are known for keeping to themselves. But if he should strike up a conversation with you whilst you are out walking, I give you permission to speak with him."

She clasped her hands together very tightly and pressed her lips to keep her smile in check. Surely he had to know that she would be spending a very great deal of time in the woods in the very near future.

May 1801

Somehow it was not surprising that a solid week of rain should follow her outing with Papa, keeping her inside and well away from any dragon meetings. Why did it always seem the weather conspired against all things desirable? Ah, well, all was not lost, though. It did give her plenty of time to transcribe the bulk of the Pendragon Treaty—the foundation of the human-dragon peace in Britain—into her commonplace book.

It was a shame, though, that she could not possibly copy those lovely medieval letters that were used in Papa's copy of the treaty. He said it was a family heirloom, dating back to the first Keeper of Longbourn and his estate. No wonder he did not want it leaving his study. Truly, it was a treasure, both for what it said and for the artistry it displayed. How had the original scribes managed to pen them so neatly and in so many colors? And the painstakingly inked dragons that paraded around the sides of the document! Just amazing. Perhaps Papa would allow her to try her hand at copying those when she became more skilled at drawing. A very good reason to see if Mama would take out that book on drawing for her from the circulating library in town.

Still, it really was not important that the letters were plain since the notes were for herself alone. And if that were the case, then it would not hurt to add a summary of it all at the end to remind herself of the high points of the treaty:

The Pendragon Treaty was penned to bring peace between the major dragons and between men and dragons. The treaty formed the Blue Order to which all major dragons and all humans who can hear dragons must belong upon pain of punitive action.

Papa had never mentioned a case where one who could hear dragons outright refused to join the Order. It was difficult to conceive of someone who would. But then again, people could be very difficult. Major dragons were smart enough to understand the great advantages the treaty offered, so they attached themselves to the Order, with only one hold-out who was later banished to the Continent. Minor dragons had the option of joining but could not vote on proceedings, much as men without Keeps could not vote.

The treaty assigned all major dragons and their progeny a territory, according to their size and needs, to be overseen by Keepers and their progeny, likewise assigned to the territory. Keepers bear the responsibility of ensuring all the Keep's dragons' needs are met. In return, major dragons foreswore all aggression toward man and dragon (except where necessary in defense of their own lives) and promised to keep order among the lesser dragons in their territory. When disputes arise, the treaty declares they are to be settled by the Blue Order Council, a group charged with maintaining the peace established by the Pendragon Treaty.

All in all, it really was simple. Why did it take so many words and pages to say it all in official terms? At least it made a very pretty—and sizeable—first entry in her commonplace book. Pray Mama never asked to read it.

The next day the rains finally broke, and Elizabeth dashed out for a walk as soon as the sun had fully risen.

Morning air was certainly the most agreeable, far nicer than that in the afternoon. Perhaps it was the fresh, dewy scent on the air and the hint of cool in the breeze. Perhaps it was the golden light of sunrise that made everything glow with a warm, welcoming feel. Perhaps it was because the birds—and the fairy dragons—were singing then, or that there were few people were out and about to question where she was going.

Whatever it was, morning walks were probably going to become a habit very soon.

Especially if it meant she could see dragons.

At the spot where the fields met the woods, she found a tree stump for a seat and peered up into the morning sky. Tiny specks that must be fairy dragons darted back and forth, catching dragonflies and other rather large insects. Surely the bugs could not taste very good, all leggy and crunchy and squishy in the middle. She shuddered a bit.

"Not all of them eat bugs, you know."

She jumped and looked down. A large striped cat face with tufted ears and bright green eyes peered up at her. His eyes were a little far-set and did not seem quite focused, but his voice was clear and sure. Perhaps the rather vacant expression was what made people think tatzelwurms stupid.

"I was not aware. I have only just begun to learn about fairy dragons from Papa."

"Odd, that is usually the first sort of dragon children are made familiar with. They are certainly the least frightening—and the most tasty." He licked his rather substantial fangs with a long, forked tongue.

That definitely did not fit in a cat's face.

But he was a tatzelwurm, not a cat, so it was most clearly appropriate.

"Pray do not tell me you eat them!" She pressed the back of her hand to her mouth.

"If you wish." He raised a thumbed paw and licked between his toes. "I am Rumblkins."

She rose and curtsied. "I am pleased to make your acquaintance. I am Elizabeth Bennet."

"You are part of the Keeper's family."

"I am his daughter."

He flicked his serpentine tail sharply. The dark smooth scales caught the morning light just so, gleaming a bit like polished metal. "Your housekeeper does not like cats."

"I do not know that Mrs. Hill dislikes them." She chewed her lip and cocked her head. "No, I am quite certain. She is quite happy to have them catching mice and rats. She detests those."

"The woman with the cap with dangling ribbons threw shoes at me." His tail lashed back and forth in the grass.

"I know no one by that description at the house. Perhaps it was a housekeeper for my father's father?"

Rumblkins wrinkled his nose. "I will not take a chance. I do not like shoes thrown at me."

"I will not throw shoes at you."

"I thought not since you are not carrying any." He sat back on his tail, as though sitting on his haunches. "Have you anything for me to eat?"

The book Papa had shown her about tatzelwurms said that they were always hungry. That much appeared very true. But it had also said that "Wyrm type dragons are considered the least intelligent and least reliable of the dragons. Of the wyrms, tatzelwurms are regarded the most capricious and least loyal. They rarely choose to be companions to Dragon Friends and when they do, they are aloof, independent and unaffectionate."

Rumblkins rubbed his face against her ankles, purring very loudly. "I smell cod. I like cod very well."

"Will you be my friend if I give you dried cod?"

"I will be your friend even if you do not. Scratch my ears." He shoved his face under her hand.

She scratched behind his ears and under his chin. His purrs grew so loud she could feel them as he rubbed against her. What a sweet creature and not aloof at all. She pulled a piece of dried cod from her apron pocket and offered it to him.

Instead of taking it in his teeth as a cat might, he took it from her with his thumbed paw and brought it to his mouth. There all semblance of manners ended, and he gobbled the fish, spittle and tiny slivers of meat flying.

Was it just tatzelwurms or were all dragons revolting when they ate? He did wash his face like a cat when he was finished, which almost, but not quite, made up for the grisly manners he had displayed.

"Why are you staring at me so?" Rumblkins asked as he licked between his thumb and toes.

"I have never been so close to a tatzelwurm before. You do not look like the drawings in the books I have seen."

He wrinkled his nose and snorted—or was that a sneeze? "I have heard that much of what has been written about dragons was written by those who could not hear."

"But if they could not hear dragons, how could those men have written about them?"

"Chance encounters still occur sometimes. Occasionally men cannot be persuaded out of what they saw. So when that happens, they are persuaded to believe they saw something much more outlandish than what they actually did. That way their accounts are as far away from the truth as possible. Then they put them in the foolish books and all manner of strange and stupid accounts are written."

Papa would certainly not like to hear that! Perhaps that is why he though Rumblkins addlepated. "I have not read that in any of the Pendragon Accords."

"It is something we have always done. I do not know why anyone would bother to have written it down."

"I suppose that makes sense." She chewed her lip. "Are you venomous?"

"Why would you think that?" His brows knit together, and he managed a very exasperated look.

"Some books say so, and you have very long fangs."

"Well, it is written wrong. No tatzelwurm has venom like a snake. Now our breath ..." He reared up and huffed in her face.

Gracious! Her eyes watered! She coughed into her hand.

"... has also been considered poison, but that is nonsense. Yours might be unpleasant, too, if you ate rats and mice all day."

"I will keep that in mind."

He wove between her feet again, purring. "Scratch again?"

He guided her to the itchiest places along his jaw and behind his ears. Were all dragons this itchy, or merely the ones who had fur as well as scales?

A squawk unlike any she had ever heard sliced the air and sent shivers down her spine.

"No! He is here!" Rumblkins dove behind her skirts, shaking.

"Who?"

"We call him Scarred. He has only one eye. A cockatrice with only one eye."

She scanned the sky as a large, winged shadow passed over them. Heavens, is that what Rustle looked like when he flew? She had never seen him in the air. The creature was huge! Wingtip to wingtip, he was broader than Papa was tall!

"Do not let him see me!" Rumblkins shuddered against her calves.

She pulled her skirt down around Rumblkins. The creature would not interfere with her. It was against the treaty to do so when she offered him no threat. "Why are you so afraid?"

"He has been known to eat tatzelwurms when he cannot find enough birds and fairy dragons to satisfy his appetite."

"Can you not simply reason with him?" She covered an exposed bit of his tail with her hand.

"One does not reason with a hungry predator. One avoids them." A snarl replaced the funny warble in his voice.

The cockatrice circled several more times, then flew off toward a flock of crows approaching from the western side of the fields.

Rumblkins peeked around her skirt. A tremor began at his head and progressed down his body all the way to the tip of his tail. "He is dreadful."

She shaded her eyes and peered into the bright sky. "Why have I never seen him before?"

"He is wild. He avoids your kind."

"Perhaps you should stay closer to the house. I am sure it would be safer for you."

Rumblkins shook his head forcefully enough that bits of spittle flew. "No. Well-aimed shoes hurt."

But certainly being attacked by a cockatrice could not be less painful. "Perhaps the barn then. Stay away from the poultry eaves, of course, but near the sheep, I think—yes, there are often rats there. The shepherds hate them. I am sure if they see you catch one, you will be most welcome."

He did not look convinced.

"Since they are well disposed to cats on the whole, I do not think it would be at all difficult for you to persuade them you are a valuable addition."

His eyes brightened, and a little purr rumbled in his throat. "If they are already fond of cats, then perhaps yes, they might be persuaded with only a little effort and a large rat." He smiled. It was odd to see such an expression on a decidedly feline face—with a forked tongue as well—but there was nothing else one could call such a look.

"Come with me, then. I shall walk home by way of the sheep fields so you shall have no further worries." She offered one last scratch before she stood.

They walked in companionable silence to the sheep fields. He purred as they went, sounding ever so much as though he were humming to himself. About halfway there he suddenly ran off. Gracious, he could spring hop very quickly! In very short order he returned, a large, thankfully quite dead rat in his jaws. Something to ensure a warm welcome among the shepherds, no doubt.

The sun hung barely above the tree tops by the time she left him among the shepherds and sheep, purring a contented thank you. She had not intended to be away from the house for so long and ran home as quickly as she could.

"How nice for you to finally join us, Miss Lizzy," Mama called from the parlor as Elizabeth hurried in.

She swallowed hard—that tone was never a good sign—and scurried to the parlor. Naturally, the room was warmer than Mama would have liked, warm enough to leave her short-tempered and cross. What joy was hers!

Aunt Phillips sat near Mama and Jane, glasses of lemonade on the table, their sewing in their laps.

"We were becoming worried as to what might have become of you." Aunt Phillips looked down her long, sharp nose. Was that how a hungry cockatrice looked at prey? She probably would not appreciate the comparison.

What Mama might say indirectly, Aunt Phillips was apt to put into concise, sharp words. Even Jane found her a trial to be around, though she would be hard-pressed to suggest more than that Aunt Phillips was very direct.

"Where have you been all day?" Aunt Phillips tapped her foot rapidly.

"I went for a walk this morning. After all the rain, it was ever so pleasant to go out. And while I was out, ah, the shepherds, I saw them and they asked me to bring word to Papa regarding the condition of the fields and a problem they have been having with rats among the lambs." There was a good bit of truth in the answer even if it left out the more interesting bits.

"Eww, rats!" Jane's face screwed up, and she trembled. How she loathed the creatures.

"I am surprised you approve of this, Sister!" Aunt Philips pressed her hand to her chest. "It is not proper that the field hands should think nothing of speaking to your daughter, sending messages through her as though she were a common dairymaid."

Mama mirrored Aunt's Phillips' posture. "Oh, Sister! It would not be the first time I have said such a thing to Mr. Bennet. But he insists she acts as his secretary. I have never seen such a thing—"

Elizabeth opened her mouth to speak but shut it again. Mama was going off on a tear and interrupting or offering one's opinion at such a time was always, always a bad idea. So she retrieved her work basket from the cabinet near the settee and sat next to Jane to sew.

Aunt Phillips' visit lasted only a quarter of an hour more. Once Mama had seen her to the door, she returned to the parlor.

"How could you have forgotten that your aunt was coming to call today? I am embarrassed, no, appalled that you could do such a thing, Elizabeth. It is truly shocking that you could be so distracted. You are too close to being a young lady to behave like this." Mama bustled to the cabinet nearest the door and yanked a book out of the topmost drawer. She flipped it open to a page about a quarter of the way through. "I insist you study this essay on proper etiquette and make notes of it in your commonplace book as you do. There will be no dinner until you have finished."

Elizabeth took the book and scurried upstairs, as much to be away from Mama's company as to get the task over with quickly. She had, after all, not eaten all day.

The evening sun shone directly through her window, warming her little room and making it bright enough to write easily. She sat at the dainty table near her window and opened her commonplace book to a fresh page, using its edge to hold open Mama's etiquette book. The open page read: Maxims and Rules for the Conduct of Young Women.

What a dreadful, dull-sounding title, but it was more a list than an essay, making it far faster and easier to read and make notes. That was something to be appreciated. Perhaps this would not be too awful a task.

It is unjust, as well as ill-natured, to take advantage

of the weakness of others.

That was one of the prime injunctions to both dragon and mankind in the Pendragon Accords. It must be good advice. Who would have thought that what applied to young women would also apply to dragons?

Sincerity is the groundwork of all that is good and valuable.

That seemed sensible as well. Certainly, it worked when King Uther met with the dragon Brenin—that is what they called their king—to create the Accords.

Civility is never a losing game; courtesy will always reproduce itself in others, and the original exhibitor will get at least as much as she gives.

Brenin Buckingham and King Uther exchanged civilities, and everyone had benefited for eight centuries since. Civility must be very, very important. That was worth thinking on further.

Never suffer anyone, under the presence of friendship, to take unbecoming liberties with you.

She giggled under her breath. Rumblkins would probably agree with this principle. According to him, it was dangerous to take liberties with a creature who might easily eat you. Maybe there was something to seeing the world in terms of predator and prey.

The character of a toad-eater, flatterer, or sycophant is truly detestable.

According to Papa, dragons detest flattery of all sorts. But where was the line between sincere compliment and toad-eating? Should she not have told Rumblkins that his fur was the softest and finest she had ever felt? He had not seemed offended when she had said it, but perhaps she should ask. It would be a shame to offend him unwittingly.

If you wish to identify a beau of quality, watch him at the dining table. Nothing indicates a well-bred man more than a proper mode of eating his dinner.

If this were true, then all dragons were probably brutes. Rumblkins was horrid when he ate, and he said that his manners were better than most. She swallowed hard. It was a sight difficult to put out of one's mind.

Remember that if you are quiet in society, you will, at least, have credit for discretion.

Or stupidity. It was difficult to be certain which was true and harder still to know how she might ever find out.

Women in every country have a greater influence than men choose to confess.

That was especially true of the Blue Order. Though Papa clearly did not approve, the Order acknowledged women were as important as Dragon Friends and Keepers as men. It was a wonder that the dragons recognized the influence of women so easily, but society did not. One more reason to like dragons very much.

The sun had almost set, but she was finally finished. Pray Mama would not demand to see what she had written and would simply take her word that the task was complete. Elizabeth hurried downstairs.

2
Chapter

The summer months passed quickly. Rumblkins' rat hunting prowess had quickly made him a favorite among the shepherds. Her provision for his safety from Scarred made her a favorite of his. So, every morning that she walked out among the fields—a daily habit by the end of the summer—he joined her for a chat and the occasional treat she managed to pilfer from the kitchens for him.

It was easy to see why tatzelwurms were regarded as addlepated and stupid. Conversations with Rumblkins tended to wander and ramble, often never concluding on the point that had been first set out upon. That aside though, if one was patient, he offered some truly interesting, and often amusing insights into the life of small minor dragons—something sorely missing from Papa's books of dragon lore. Not that he considered the oversight significant, but she did.

It seemed Rumblkins knew all the local forest, rock, and river wyrms and the leading fairy dragons of the harem. According to him, it was well-known in the region that he was a confirmed ratter and not fond of eating smaller dragons. Though it was the way of the world, he said, he much preferred a dinner with whom he could not share a conversation with first. Made it much faster to get to the eating when your meal did not argue with you. Yes, it was an odd sentiment, but it did facilitate his making a wide circle of acquaintances and friends.

And a wide circle he did have. He introduced her to all that would make her acquaintance. Not all wild-hatched dragons, it seemed, were accepting of warm-blooded acquaintances. But, with an introduction from Rumblkins, a surprising amount were, so she spent a great many summer hours amongst the wyrms and fairy dragons of the estate.

The rest of her hours, it seemed, were spent studying the books Papa continued to push on her. Learning what they contained was a necessary step, he said, in readying herself to meet dragons in general and Longbourn in specific.

Somehow, it did not seem to be a wise thing to mention the number of dragons she had already met without the benefit of his books. That was not the sort of thing Papa was likely to deal well with. He did not like the unexpected, and her new circle of acquaintances would definitely qualify as unexpected.

He also did not like it when she asked too many questions, especially those which appeared to contradict dragon lore. Like when the books talked about dragons, all dragons—except for fairy dragons who were just too stupid to know any better—being solitary creatures. This was so, according to the texts, because bigger dragons were predatory upon other smaller dragons, and it was unnatural for predator and prey to form any sort of relationship. Moreover, by disposition, dragons tended to be rather stubborn, self-focused, and demanding, additional traits that did not make them companionable to others of their kind.

Rumblkins though, seemed to defy all of those descriptions, being friendly, gregarious, and—what did one call a personable dragon? Dragonable? He loved to be scratched and petted and regularly sought her out for such delights. Was it possible that he was just a single exception to the entire canon of dragon lore? Or was it conceivable that dragon lore might not be entirely correct?

She winced just thinking about it. Papa would not react well to hearing that sort of thing. No, not at all.

Near the beginning of September, Papa called her into his study, a new pile of papers on his desk. It was rather surprising that she could tell that it was a new pile, considering the number of papers and journals and books that were already there. Though Mama insisted the house be kept tidy and everything put in its place, Papa's study remained the notable exception to that rule.

Ever unkempt, piles of books that he was reading, maps and scrolls he was studying, and journals he was writing in—or at least trying to write in—always seemed to cover every horizontal surface in the room, and part of the floor. One day Elizabeth had made the mistake of trying to tidy up and Papa—well, there was no other way to describe it—he became rather unhinged. There was, at least in his mind, a method to the clutter and woe to any who disturbed it. Lesson learned—she never moved another item in his study thereafter. Learning to gingerly sidestep the clutter took some doing, but it was well worthwhile.

"Have you finished your studies of the last volume I gave you?" He did not look up from the pages he was studying at his desk.

"*The Habits and Habitats of Rock-Dwelling Dragons with a Most Helpful Index to the Major Dragons of Those Types and Their Genealogies Since Pendragon's Time?*" It was hard not to giggle at the length and pretentiousness of the titles writers of dragon lore used.

Papa glanced up at her. His stern gaze suggested he did not see the same humor in them.

"Yes, sir, I have finished."

He tapped the new pile of papers on his desk. "I have been corresponding with a member of the Blue Order who believes he might be in possession of some heretofore unknown genealogies."

"Which ones? Oh, that is very exciting news!" Truthfully, it was probably more exciting to him than it was to her, but it was interesting nonetheless.

Though they did tend to be awfully dry and dull, there were times one could wheedle out some quite fascinating tidbits from genealogies. Like how long it took for different species to hatch, which types seemed apt to hibernate and for what sort of provocation, any number of things Papa did not find proper to glean from reading genealogies—all inference and no substance, he said.

"I need to travel to Loxdale Green to meet with a Mr. Garland, an apothecary with a shop by the name of Bedlow's. The Blue Order has asked that I examine the documents to determine their authenticity."

Gracious, if Papa would be traveling to see them, they must be very important documents, maybe tracing the lines of high-ranking or even royal dragon lines. He did not like to travel. Detested was the word he most often used to describe the activity.

"Mr. Garland has already made it clear that he will not allow them out of his possession. So if they are, as the Order believes, genuine, then they must be copied."

Copied? Elizabeth bit her lip. These would clearly be important documents, and she never wrote important things for him. Did that mean—

"I fear I must have help to transcribe them if necessary."

"Will the Order be sending someone to assist you?" She held her breath.

"If I ask, I am sure they would do so. But young scribes are, in general, a noxious bunch: noisy, talkative, and intrusive. I would rather not have one if it can be avoided."

She clasped her hands tightly and bit her lip.

"It seems questionable, at best, to bring someone so young. But you know not to talk too much, and I need not adjust my schedule for your convenience."

A tiny squeal escaped her lips before she could contain it.

"But, I am not yet convinced. I know you are able to conduct yourself appropriately. Your mother has seen to that. But while there, we will come into contact with a very young dragon, a minor drake just six weeks from the shell. I must be certain that you will conduct yourself appropriately in his company."

"A baby dragon? I might meet a baby dragon." She whispered the words very softly and very slowly lest she sound too pleased or excited by the prospect. But a baby dragon! Her insides bounced like Rumblkins through the fields.

"I am glad you are showing appropriate respect for the situation, but that is not enough. Prove to me that you have adequately learned what I set you to these last months, and I shall consider bringing you along."

"How shall I do that, Papa? Do you wish me to write something?"

"No, that will take far too long and require me to read it. My eyes are tired, and I would just as soon rest them for the trip." He set his glasses aside and rubbed his eyes with thumb and forefinger. "I will test you as the Blue Order does when a potential member is presented. That will be good practice for you."

She would be a member of the Blue Order someday, or at least have the chance of it? She grabbed the edge of his desk. That was a pleasure she had never really considered. Of course, it made sense as she heard dragons and was the daughter of a Keeper, but still, it felt rather surprising to hear it spoken aloud.

Pray he had no more surprises for her. Any more might render her fully unable to speak.

"So then, Lizzy, tell me how dragons are ranked."

She swallowed hard. It was a tricky question. "Dragons are ranked first by their size and power. All the major dragons, those bigger than a large horse—" That was an odd designation, but, especially now, it seemed better to keep that opinion to her commonplace book. "—outrank all the minor dragons and major dragons smaller than themselves. The major dragons are like our upper class and the minor dragons like the lower ones. Among the major dragons, the most powerful species are above the weaker ones."

Hmmm, in a number of dragon species the females were as large and powerful as the males, sometimes even more so. Perhaps that was why dragons were so easily accepting of human females—they were after all, not usually that different in size than males, not by dragon standards in any case, and thus not assumed to be of lower rank. What an interesting thought.

Papa nodded, just a little. Clearly, he was not going to comment on the success of her answers in the midst of the "test." By the way he held his shoulders, though, he seemed pleased.

"How and why were dragons' ranks established?"

"The Pendragon Accords established the ranks for the major dragons so they would no longer fight for precedence. Before the Accords, they battled for position and territory. In those days, dragon wars were almost constant. The damage to both man and dragon was unimaginable."

Papa grunted. Surely that meant she answered correctly.

"Who is the highest-ranked dragon in England?"

"The dragons of England are led by their Brenin, Buckingham. He is like our king. A firedrake, he administers dragon law and the Pendragon Accords across England and deals with necessary matters with dragons of other lands." While this was probably good to know, what did it have to do with meeting a young minor drake?

"What ranks make up the dragon equivalent of our peerage and what are their responsibilities?"

"The Dugs and Duges, who are the females, sit on the Council and lead the Dragon Conclave with their Keepers. They administer the different counties and decide matters of dragon law. Cownts and Cowntesses serve under the Dugs. They are responsible for regions in their counties, managing the major dragons and their keepers there. And so it goes down through the Vikonts and Vicontes, the Barwins and Barwines, Marchogs and Marchoes down to the lowly Lairds and Lairdas who are the lowest of the major dragons. They are the gentlemen and ladies among the dragons and are responsible for managing the minor dragons of their Keeps."

His brows creased, but the lines around his eyes remained soft. Why did he try to appear so severe if she was actually doing quite well? Why did he have to be so perplexing? She held her breath not to sigh. He did not like it when she sighed.

"What type of dragon has wings?" He avoided meeting her gaze.

"That is a trick question, sir. Dragons are typed by the shape of their heads, not their appendages. Amphitheres are a snake-type dragon with wings. All the bird types, all species of cockatrice and fairy dragons, have wings. Firedrakes and wyverns, who are dragon types, also have wings."

"What snake-type dragon has both major and minor species?"

"The basilisk. They are also the only snake-type to have four legs." The way his eyes narrowed—maybe it was not a good idea to offer more information than he asked. So mentioning that wyrms and drakes also had major and minor species was out of the question.

"What are the weakest type of dragon and the strongest?"

"Wyrm-types are on the whole the weakest and dragon-types the strongest, even though the wyvern is one of the weakest species."

Papa grumbled under his breath. Perhaps he did not like being reminded that their estate dragon was among the least powerful and lowest ranking in the kingdom. "Tell me about lizard types."

"Some have argued that dragon types should really be called lizard types for the shape of their heads—and often the rest of them as well—resemble large lizards. But it is a very great insult to suggest a dragon resembles a lizard and an even greater insult to call a dragon a big lizard. Such an insult was once considered a breach of the Pendragon Treaty and sufficient provocation to acquit the offended drake of assault against the man who said it."

He did not even blink. "Which dragon type has no major dragon species?"

"Bird types, or so it is believed, however—"

A sharp, staccato knock rang out from the door. Mama's.

Papa squeezed his eyes shut and pressed his temples. "Come in."

Mama bustled in, fluffed like the top hen in the henhouse looking for someone to peck. That did not bode well at all. "So this is where you have been hiding, Lizzy."

Papa sat up very straight and rapped his desk with his knuckles. "She has not been hiding. I have called her here myself."

"Well, it is time for her to go to practice her pianoforte. My sister Phillips will be by tomorrow to hear her play. I want Lizzy's piece to be perfect for her."

"I did practice earlier, Mama, before breakfast." Jane had even commented about how much improved her playing was.

"I did not hear you."

Elizabeth bit her lip. Reminding her that she slept very soundly when she had taken the draught the apothecary had left her was not a politic thing to bring up.

"Go, go now. I have something I wish to speak to your father about."

"Wait, Lizzy. I want you to go upstairs right now and pack your carpetbag." Papa pushed up from his desk.

"Pack her bag? Whatever for?" Mama stood between her and the door.

"I have business that will take me from Longbourn for a few days."

"What has that to do with our daughter?"

"The business will entail no small amount of writing." He waved Elizabeth toward the door.

Mama blocked her way again. "It is not proper that you should have Lizzy involved in your business dealings. It is not proper for a young lady. Surely, you can see that."

"What would you suggest instead?"

"Hire a man, a steward, a secretary, someone. It would be far more proper than your daughter."

"Mrs. Bennet." He spoke her name in a certain particular way which said so much more than he could speak in simple words, especially in front of Elizabeth. "I have shown you the estate books. You know precisely why that is not an option."

"It is always about numbers to you, cold, unfeeling man." She pressed a handkerchief to her nose. Pray she did not try to cry now. It was always an unseemly show.

"Numbers do not have feelings. They represent facts, and the fact is that you have made the choice that I shall not have a secretary. If you wish to change that, then it is well within your power to do so."

Mama snorted. "Oh, very well then, when you put it in those terms! At least you should take Jane with you, not Lizzy. If you need something written, Jane is a much better choice. Her hand is prettier than Lizzy's."

Elizabeth bit her lip. Mama was right on that point. Clearly, that was an excellent reason to improve her penmanship, one that until this moment had never occurred to her.

"I need legible writing, not pretty." Papa waved her away. "Go to your room now, Lizzy."

She scurried out and closed the door behind her. Unfortunately, her room was directly above the study. The preternatural hearing that allowed her to perceive dragon speech could be a disadvantage at times, especially when there were things one did not want to hear.

"You know I am a very capable writer. My hand is very neat," Mama said in her best wheedling tone. "I should like very much to travel and meet new people."

No doubt Papa was rolling his eyes. "Perhaps if there were money for a governess—"

"Hill is quite capable of caring for the girls for a few days."

"My trip is one of business, not pleasure. There will be little opportunity to socialize. You would not appreciate being confined to a library all day, transcribing the records that I need."

"How do you know that?"

"Just last week, you became impatient copying a receipt from the book Lady Lucas lent you. How could you tolerate pages and pages of copying?"

"You underestimate me. You do not appreciate me." Mama sniffled to punctuate the accusation.

"I know you very well and copying, especially accurate copying, is not your forte. You would be miserable in minutes. I must get this business done without interruption."

Mama grumbled, but she could hardly argue Papa's point. "At least bring Jane. She would appreciate the experience. She is older and more deserving of it than Lizzy."

"Jane's hand may be very neat, but she is very much like you. I have found her writing to be inaccurate. Moreover, she is distracted too easily."

"How can you find fault with her sweet disposition? Everyone likes her, for she is the dearest girl."

Everyone but dragons. They did not seem to care very much about her one way or the other.

Papa brought his foot down sharply. "I do not need a dear girl to chaperone. I need someone who can copy and write for me exactly as I need them to without wanting to run off for amusements. The only person in this house capable of that is Lizzy."

"I do not understand why you must play such favorites among our girls." Now Mama was crying. When would she realize that would never move Papa to a favorable opinion?

Perhaps if she dragged her table to the far side of the room and wrote in her commonplace book, she could distract herself from the conversation heating up below her. Rumblkins had introduced her to a new pair of rock wyrms recently—little wyrms always seemed to travel in mated pairs. That was not something she had seen in dragon lore, at least not yet. That was worth writing about, especially the funny way their pairs interacted, finishing each other's sentences as they twined around each other. Often it resulted in utter nonsense, but even that was an interesting observation.

An hour later, the door of her room creaked open, and Papa peeked in, weary and shoulders stooped. "Pack your carpetbag, Lizzy. I want to leave on the hour."

"Yes, Papa!" She jumped up and ran for the closet, her heart beating faster than it ever had before. She would be going on her first journey, and a dragon would be at the end of it! What more could she ever have wished for?

September 1801

It was odd to have an entire seat of the carriage to herself, no one blocking her view or the fresh breeze that danced in on the sunshine through the open side glass. Usually, Elizabeth was crowded in with her sisters squashed in on either side. Today, she had to brace on her own against the sway and jolt of the coach as each bump transmitted through the thin squabs. Who would think she would be missing their presence when she had all this lovely space to herself?

Papa sat across from her, eyes lightly closed, not quite sleeping, but lost in his own thoughts. So quiet and still, he almost blended into the dry cracked leather seats and scuffed finishes. Mama was ever after him to have the carriage refitted; it had been his father's, after all. But he only consented to necessary repairs. Until now, it had seemed a matter of economy that he did so. But he seemed so comfortable here, perhaps there was an element of nostalgia as well.

He did not appreciate constant conversation during a carriage ride, ignoring it when he could not avoid it altogether. That might have made it a lonely journey except for the lovely large leather-bound book in her lap. Papa had brought that particular tome of dragon lore along, knowing how much she had yearned to read it. Had it been any ordinary book, her pride might have been offended that he thought she needed to be bribed into silence. But *Dragon Etiquette Volume 1: Greetings* was a prize worth setting aside pride for, especially considering how rarely he allowed his books out of his study.

Given she would meet her first dragon outside the confines of Longbourn's Keep on this trip, studying dragon greetings was a very fitting thing. Bedlow was just a baby, though, but Papa assured her that, even at such a tender age, Bedlow would be able to walk and talk—and take offense—just as an older dragon might. Even so, he was unlikely to be very particular about proper manners.

That was just as well, though. Dragon greetings were rather complex. No, not rather, they were very complex. Very, very complex. Surely it would be easier to be presented before the King. At least at court, there were fewer nuances to be considered.

With dragons, so much depended on dominance, whether or not it was already established. Were those who were meeting of the same species or not? If they were of the same species, would they honor the established species hierarchy? After all, frilled minor drakes were loath to recognize that horned minor drakes ranked above them, so much so that they would regularly fight to prove themselves dominant. Were wings, frills, fins, or hoods involved? Tails, feathers, puffing one's body out, stances, even scents all could play a role.

She rubbed her eyes with her fists. How was one to remember it all for each different species and every possible combination of species? Moreover, how was she to properly communicate with dragons when she lacked the capacity to express the correct body language?

Obviously, members of the Blue Order accomplished that and had for some time. More or less, anyway. But so many attempted greetings ended in misunderstanding, sometimes of a tragic variety. Could there not be a better way to convey a greeting more accurately?

Perhaps there could be some sort of substitute for those body parts she was not blessed with—a fan or a large hat, perhaps. No, that would be silly. She giggled under her breath. A coat … or a cloak! That might be very good. She pulled her commonplace book and pencil from her carpetbag and jotted a quick reminder. Perhaps she might try her hand at a few sketches later when Papa did not require her assistance.

A very full cloak could act like wings or a puffed body if handled correctly. It would require some form of straps inside to permit that. And an ample hood could extend out like a frill if the edges were stiffened properly, or cover her face when necessary to show deference. It all made a great deal of sense …

"Lizzy? Lizzy, are you paying attention? We have arrived. Arrange your bag now so we can debark." Papa reached for his satchel.

She jumped and slipped both books into her bag. How delightful Papa had not asked for his volume back. Hopefully, she could continue her study later tonight.

Papa handed her out of the carriage in front of a large apothecary's shop with a thatched roof and weathered wooden sideboards. Attractive displays filled the front window that kept watch over a neatly swept porch. A sign above the door bore the silhouette of a dragon on one side and an apothecary jar on the other and read *Bedlow's* in large red letters.

How odd. The proprietor was Mr. Garland. Should not the place be called Garland's? Perhaps merchants named their establishments for their Dragon Friends as Keeps were named for their territorial dragons.

Papa led her to the door. What a very friendly-looking place it seemed. Her heart raced just a mite. There was a drakling to meet just inside. Would he be friendly? Would he like her?

A round, red man flung open the door and beckoned them inside. Everything about him was rosy: his cheeks, his nose, his hair, his mustache, even his apron was a faded red. It was all a happy sort of gingery-red, not the angry sort of short-tempered red that some people wore like a scowl. He had a funny sort of trundle-waddle step as he showed them through his tidy shop to a sitting room upstairs through a cloud of herbal scents tinged with just a hint of dragon musk.

"You must forgive me. My sister who keeps house for me is away right now." Mr. Garland bowed over his round belly as they entered the sitting room.

The room was only half the size of Mama's sitting room, a bit crowded and cluttered and dark. Not gloomy, precisely, but dark in the way rooms were when the occupant had more interesting things to do than clean rooms. A bit like Papa's study.

"May I present my daughter, Elizabeth? She has come to be my scribe today." Papa nodded at her, and she curtsied.

Mr. Garland's eyes grew wide. "She knows about the …"

Papa patted her shoulder. "She hears and already knows quite a bit about dragons."

Mr. Garland heaved a little sigh that sounded relieved. "Very good. I hate the thought of keeping Bedlow away. The little fellow is too young to be left on his own for very long."

What a very dear fellow, so concerned for his little Friend. It was easy to like Mr. Garland very much, even just a few moments after meeting him. There was something very trustworthy in someone who cared so for a dragon.

"Bring him out. We will both be charmed to meet him." Papa shuffled toward the nearest chair, a frayed and faded wingback. Elizabeth perched on a stool beside him.

That brought a huge smile to Mr. Garland's face, and he shuffled out. A short moment later, he returned with a bundle the size of one of Papa's pointers wrapped in a tattered blanket. He crouched down, and his burden spilled out of his arms in a tangle of limbs and frayed wool. A little red drake—of course, he would have to be red to match his Friend!—tumbled out onto the floor.

It was a struggle not to laugh. He righted himself on all fours and shook as though to get everything in the right places again. About the size of a hunting dog, he was hardly alarming, especially because of his baby proportions. His deep blue eyes were far too large for his face, wide and innocent, but that would soon be replaced by mischief, no doubt. His feet were too big for his body, rather like a puppy, and his tail far too long. In short, he was adorable.

She crouched down and dipped her head in a greeting of equals—they were both children, after all. He toddled up to her and touched his nose to hers. It was cold and smooth and dry.

"I Bedlow."

"And I am Elizabeth. Shall I scratch your ears?"

He stretched his neck toward her in a clear invitation. She scratched behind his ears the way that Rumblkins most liked. She had become so accustomed to scratching a furry dragon that Bedlow's smooth cool scales felt a bit odd. Not unpleasant, but odd.

Bedlow cooed and thumped his tail. He turned his side to her for more scratching. Apparently, what was pleasant for fur was also pleasing for scales. Mr. Garland's smile stretched into a hearty grin.

Were all dragons itchy? It seemed like Rumblkins always was and now Bedlow. That was probably something she should write down. Bedlow wound around her like a cat, rubbing his face against her legs.

Papa reached down to pat his head. The drakling met him halfway, tail thumping. "What a fine little fellow he is."

"He is a grand young thing for sure." Mr. Garland joined them near the floor and scratched under Bedlow's chin. "But the poor lad seems rather sulky at the moment. I think his teeth be bothering him. I 'spect I will need to call the surgeon to lance his gums if he don't get better soon. I hate to do it, but none of the dragon lore has any better notions."

"Is teething in dragons as dangerous as teething in human babies?" She turned to Papa. "The Lucas' baby boy nearly died of teething even though his gums were lanced by the best surgeon in Meryton. Poor little chap." Her stomach tightened as she chewed her knuckle.

"I am not sure anyone knows for certain, but we

always take all the precautions we can for the comfort and safety of our friends." Papa leaned back with a pained look. Was that for the dragon or for his own discomfort?

Mr. Garland leaned toward her and looked her directly in the eye. "Do you know anything about babies, young miss? I know young women often do. If you know anything to comfort him …"

"I will try to remember what was done for the Lucas boy, but in any case, I can sit with him and keep him company whilst you and Papa talk." Bedlow rubbed his jaw hard against her knee, hard enough to hurt a bit. A gobbet of drool trickled down the edge of his mouth.

Poor baby must be very uncomfortable.

"He can show you around the house if he would like. That might give him a few moments' distraction." Mr. Garland rubbed the sides of Bedlow's face and wiped the spittle away with his apron. "Would you like to show your new friend the old place?"

"Come. I show." Bedlow gently took her wrist in his mouth and pulled her toward the door.

"Go along, Lizzy. I will call for you when you are needed."

She struggled to contain her smile as she scurried along after Bedlow. Papa trusted her alone with a new dragon friend!

He led her to the narrow wooden stairs, his talons clacking on the steps as he walked, and down to the dim kitchen with only a single window. A cheery fire crackled near a large basket on the hearth. Lingering scents of old stew and baking bread filled the stone walls with a comfortable sense of home.

"Do you sleep there?" She pointed at the basket.

"It warm. I like warms." He sat hard on the stone

floor and pawed at his mouth. "I no like this."

"May I see?" She sat next to him.

"Can make stop?" He cocked his head, a bit of drool sliding from the corner of his wide mouth down his neck. "Itches, hurts, burns. I no like."

"Open your mouth and promise not to bite me." On second thought, putting her hand in a dragon's mouth might not be a good idea.

Bedlow's jaw swung open surprisingly wide. Gracious, just how large was his mouth? Just behind his baby fangs, his gums were swollen red and angry-looking. Poor baby!

"Do not bite me." She reached inside and rubbed her fingertips along his gums firmly like she had seen Lady Lucas do with her baby.

Bedlow started and nearly clamped down but stopped just in time. She would definitely think twice about putting her hand in a dragon's mouth again!

He leaned into her hand. "Dat gud," he murmured through her fingers, eyelids drooping and eyes rolling back.

Baby Lucas had liked the same thing. Hmmm, Lady Lucas had given him something to put in his mouth, a stick of some sort … no … wait, it was a coral! A family heirloom of some kind. He would gum it, and it made him feel better, for a short time at least.

Well, that would not do—even if Mr. Garland had such an heirloom, there was little chance it was big enough for that mouth!

Bedlow sat on the hearth and moved from her fingers to gumming her wrist—just a bit too hard for her liking. Ouch. But he cooed so happily as he did it, how could she possibly stop him?

Clearly, the little drake needed something to chew

on, but what? Wood would splinter, pewter was too hard and could puncture, a knotted rag soaked in sugar or even rum would shred too easily, not to mention that few dragons tolerated liquor well. A horseshoe would be too hard, so would bricks or stone.

He released her wrist for a moment, and she rose to pace the length of the kitchen. Sometimes the movement helped to shake a thought or two loose.

Bedlow trotted after her like a puppy, whining softly. "No go, please no go." He butted her with the top of his head.

"I am right here." She reached down to scratch his ears. He really was much like a large puppy … that was it! Puppies chewed bones!

Surely there would be a large bone somewhere in a kitchen that smelt like stew. She scanned the room. There, in a large bowl, probably destined for soup. Hopefully, Mr. Garland would not mind—though his cook probably would. But he had said she could try to soothe Bedlow if she could.

She hurried over to the bone and carefully lifted it from the bowl, brushing vegetable trimmings away as she did.

Bedlow rose up on his back legs and sniffed what she was doing. "Smells good. Like dinner."

Was he always hungry like Rumblkins, too?

"Here. I think it will feel good on your gums. Chew it like you were doing with my wrist." She carried the bone to his hearth basket and encouraged him to climb in. Even if the bone did not help, at least he would be somewhere comfortable.

His eyebrows knit, but he kept the question to himself, probably because the meat left clinging to the bone smelt too good to refuse. He curled up in the basket and took the bone from her hand.

Naturally, he ignored her instructions and picked all the meat off first and licking it well for good measure. Only after his snack was finished—it seemed there were few things dragons liked better than eating—did he begin to chew as she directed. He whimpered and complained at first, slowly getting used to the sensation. Then he went after the beef shank with enthusiasm. A few minutes later, he rolled onto his back to hold the bone with all four dexterous feet as he chewed, the tip of his red tail flicking happily. He rumbled to himself, a happy purry sort of sound.

"Well, I'll be…"

Elizabeth jumped and turned. Mr. Garland and Papa stood in the doorway.

"I have been calling for you for at least five minutes complete." Papa scowled just a little.

"Never mind that! What have you done?" Mr. Garland trundled over to the hearth basket. "The little chap has not looked this happy since this business with his teeth began. Look at him."

"Like bone! Feel good!" Bedlow grinned up at Mr. Garland, tail wagging happily.

Mr. Garland scratched the drakling's pale belly. "You may have all the bones you like. I will put an order in with the butcher directly." He looked up at Papa. "I think I will hold off calling that surgeon."

"As long as the relief continues, I do not see why not." His features softened just a mite. He was pleased after all.

"Why is there nothing of this in dragon lore? It seems so very simple a solution." Mr. Garland balanced his fists on his hips.

"I have no idea. Perhaps no one thought to take

note of it. It does seem a very basic, simple sort of thing." Papa glanced at Elizabeth, one eyebrow cocked.

"You will, Miss, write this down for me, and anything else you can think of for his comfort—in between copying for your father, of course. Will you not?" Mr. Garland extended an open hand to her.

"I should be most happy to."

"I expect we shall be here several days, Lizzy. Do start by writing a letter to your mother to inform her of that. Come upstairs to the office. There is a writing desk waiting for you."

She rose; Bedlow jumped up after her, carrying his bone in his mouth. He trotted upstairs to the office and curled around her feet, gnawing happily. His hide was warm from the fire and felt so cozy around her ankles.

Mama might grumble about them being gone for several days, but Papa seemed to like Mr. Garland's company and really, what could be much better than days spent learning new dragon genealogies with a new dragon friend to keep company with?

If this was what Blue Order Business was like, pray Papa would invite her along very often!

3
Chapter

October 1801

Returning home after nearly a week spent in Bedlow's company proved far more heart-wrenching than she could have ever anticipated. Baby dragons were absolutely endearing and very difficult to part from. Rejoining a household without a dragon gave a whole new meaning to the words *empty* and *lonely*. How could Papa possibly tolerate having no household Dragon Friend? It seemed entirely unnatural.

Although, if one considered it, the argument could be made, at least among those who did not hear, that having a household dragon was a far more unnatural state than having one. But that was a largely academic point, better saved for more philosophical times.

Papa remained unmoved. With so many in the family unable to hear dragons, having one in the house would be untenable at best. Dragons were capricious, independent creatures, he insisted, not likely to respect the delicate situation he was in. Dragon mischief would no doubt put the household in constant strife. And no, a dragon's persuasive ability over those who could not hear them would not likely make it any better.

He was entirely resolved, so she kept her opinions to herself and spent a great deal of time in the fields with Rumblkins.

One cool, clear autumn morning—the kind that was crisp and invited one to run along the fences as fast as she could—Mama insisted Elizabeth go out to the fading flower garden. Cutting flowers for the house was indeed a crucial task for an eleven-year-old young lady, clearly deserving of Elizabeth's full attention. Wandering outside in the fresh air and crisp breezes was certainly not something to complain about. But when she was done, she would be expected inside to sit through another interminable lesson in the art of arranging flowers.

It was difficult to think of something she cared about less. Very difficult indeed. Though perhaps the art of small talk appropriate for a morning social call was even less interesting. Regardless, the process seemed to please Mama, so in that, it was a worthy endeavor. But truly, in the larger scheme of things, it all seemed rather silly.

Elizabeth snipped another fluffy yellow flower—what was the name of it? Several petals shook loose and floated to the ground as she tucked it into her basket. Somehow it was far easier to remember the various dragon species and their distinctions than these silly flowers. She sniffled and rubbed her itchy nose against her sleeve. Foolish flowers!

Still though, the entire affair had one very great advantage to it, so much so that she felt little need to find a way to escape the task. Sometimes, if she was very lucky, a pair of fairy dragons flitted among the flowers. Occasionally, when she put out a saucer with honey and preserves, they stopped to gorge themselves on her offerings, allowing her time to study the delightful tiny creatures.

Usually, they were mistaken for hummingbirds or other small songbirds, but that only made the wee creatures all the more delightful. Brightly-colored gems among the dull garden plants with sweet songs that left one feeling soft and easy.

This pair proved particularly bold and friendly. They permitted her close enough to make detailed observations. Already she had drawn several meticulous images of their wings and feet and eyes. Once, the larger male left a lovely lavender feather scale behind which she pressed in her commonplace book—a treasure she could hardly set a value upon. It was pleasant to think it might have been left in thanks for the saucer of honey she had brought them.

Another time, they flew chittering circles around her head, their voices so high and words so fast she could hardly understand them, but what she had understood was complimentary. It seemed they were grateful for the way she had chased a hunting tomcat away from them.

Perhaps she might see them today. That would make cutting all these silly, sneezy flowers worthwhile. It was not likely, though, not this late in the season. Usually in the autumn, according to Papa's dragon lore, they would be busy making warm nests in which to spend the winter.

Unlike the larger dragons who could tolerate the frigid weather, insulated against the temperatures in their underground lairs, fairy dragons heartily disliked the cold and tried to sleep through the winter season in nests built in tree hollows that they shared with one another. Or so the books said; sometimes they were wrong. Maybe this would be one of those days.

She crouched down to cut a stem near the ground.

"Mrrow." A fuzzy head bumped her elbow and nearly made her drop her scissors. Rumblkins wove around her ankles and purred.

"Good afternoon to you." She extended her hand, and he rubbed himself against it, giving her permission to pet his luxurious fur.

The tatzelwurm sported long, striped fur on his feline front half while his back, snake-like half was covered in dark, sleek scales. Mama and her sisters were persuaded he was a large farm cat. How very surprised they would be to discover he was a small dragon.

"What brings you to the flower garden? Pray tell me we do not have a family of rats living here!" She jumped back a bit—rats were truly horrid creatures.

"No, no rats. I ate them." He sat back on his haunches and licked his thumbed paw. Such funny feet he had. "But there is something in the woods I think you and your father would want to know."

She gasped and dropped her scissors. "What is wrong?"

"Oh, nothing is wrong. Everything is perfectly normal and natural."

She tucked her scissors under the flowers in her basket and sighed softly. "But then, why have you come to talk to me?"

"It is something I think you will want to know, not something that is wrong." The tufted tips of his ears flicked.

There was a reason why tatzelwurms had a reputation for being a bit daft.

"Pray tell me then what normal and natural things might my father and I find interesting?"

"There is a pair of fairy dragons that you have been watching in the garden." He glanced up as though they might appear at any moment.

Now that could be significant indeed. Pray nothing had happened to them. "A purple male and a green female?"

"Yes, them." He licked his shoulder as though he had suddenly lost his train of thought. "They have been preparing their winter nest with the rest of the purple one's harem. They completed it several days ago."

She peered over her shoulder into the woods. "Will you show me where their winter nest is?"

"I can, but I hardly think that is the thing you would be interested in."

Tatzelwurms required a great deal of patience.

She forced her face into a smile. "Even more intriguing. Pray tell me."

"The pair had another nest you see—one with eggs." Rumblkins licked his lips and smacked his jaws.

"Is it not late in the season for fairy dragon eggs?"

Rumblkins rose up on his haunches. "Indeed, those flitterbobs made a muck of things and waited too long to take their mating flight. They have laid their eggs far too late. Now the eggs are in the nest, but the brood parents have gone away to keep snug for the cold season. The eggs are alone and near to hatching. Just this morning, I saw a weasel sniffing around the tree with the nest. Your father said he wanted to know of abandoned eggs. He promised me—"

"Dried cod, yes, I remember him telling me. Come to the house with me, and I shall tell Papa straight away. He will bring you some cod. I am sure he will want you to show him where the eggs are. I think he will want to rescue them."

Rumblkins licked his lips, purring, and followed her to the house in his funny spring-and-hop way. It really was one of the oddest forms of locomotion one could imagine. It was easy to see how some believed it addled their brains to bounce around so much. There were times it seemed entirely likely.

Elizabeth gave her flower basket to Mama and insisted she needed to deliver an urgent message to Papa and only Papa. She dashed off to look for him, but he was neither in his book room nor in his room upstairs. Mrs. Hill finally revealed that he was gone into the village on business and was not expected back until near dinnertime.

Botheration! What a time for him to be away. Those eggs were in danger and might well not survive the day left alone with a weasel in the vicinity. What was she to do? The Blue Order made it very clear: it was a Dragon Keeper's duty to preserve dragon life wherever possible. She had to do something to try to save those eggs.

But how? She was only a girl. What could she possibly do?

She detoured through the bustling kitchen where Cook and her staff were already busy with dinner preparations and rooted through the pantry for a dry cod—conveniently to be found in a wooden box on a low shelf. Rumblkins sat nearby, whispering to the cook, the maid, and Mrs. Hill that there was nothing notable whatsoever going on. There was no reason to ask why or to even notice Elizabeth in the kitchen at all. And most of all, there was no cat in the kitchen.

Elizabeth had never really seen dragon persuasion enacted before. It was difficult to tell what was more interesting, watching him tell Longbourn's staff what to think, or them pausing with peculiar looks on their faces, considering what the little dragon was saying. Then they muttered to themselves something that sounded very much like what Rumblkins had told them, and went about their business once more.

Did everyone respond to persuasion that way, or was it peculiar to Longbourn alone? Perhaps one day she would have the opportunity to see that for herself.

With the staff amply distracted, Elizabeth took a large cod from the box and led Rumblkins outside.

Stubborn creature insisted on gobbling down the entire fish before he was willing to show her the tree with the nest. Just how long could it take a tatzelwurm to eat a single fish?

Apparently, quite some time when he enjoyed it as much as Rumblkins appeared to love cod. He savored each bite, licked his paws, Elizabeth's hands, and the step where she had placed the fish. Was he trying to be frustrating?

"Will you take me to the nest now?"

"Will you give me another fish when we return?" He balanced on his serpentine tail and bumped her elbow with the top of his head.

"If the eggs come back safely with me, you will have two fish."

He rubbed himself around her ankles and between her feet, purring. "Mrrow, come." He leapt off in the direction of the woods. Elizabeth ran to keep up with him.

Although she had wandered the woods on Longbourn estate often on her own, this particular part of the woods was unfamiliar and technically forbidden. Old hardwoods grew thick here, casting deep shade over the loamy ground surrounding a large, rocky hillside. Generally, she preferred a place with more sunlight, but these woods were pleasant enough, even rather peaceful.

Papa said these woods were the explicit territory of the wyvern Longbourn. A dragon's territory was always to be respected—and avoided until one gained an invitation. As major dragons went, wyverns were considered small and relatively insignificant, among the least powerful of the major dragon species. Still, a major dragon was a very powerful and not entirely predictable creature. Papa insisted she was not to go there until she had been properly introduced and received by him. Until then, he might consider her a trespasser, and it could end badly for them all.

It would be best to obey Papa, but these were very unusual circumstances. Dragon lives were at stake. There was no time to waste waiting for him to return. She had to protect those babies!

Should Longbourn appear, surely he would understand and grant her passage through the woods of her father's own estate. It only made sense that the estate dragon would be a reasonable soul. He was after all responsible for the territory and should welcome her help. Why would he not?

Rumblkins ran deeper and deeper into the shady woods. Each springy hop propelled him a very great length—as if he had legs as long as a horse! For his odd means of locomotion, he was amazingly fast! Just how far back did these woods extend? Pray Rumblkins would not leave her! She might not be able to find her way back.

At long last, he stopped near a very tall tree. She leaned hard against it, panting to catch her breath. This was the farthest she had ever walked alone, and perhaps the fastest! Foot prints and a tuft of red-brown fur lay near the tree. Stoats, several of them. One of Papa's books said that fairy dragon eggs were a special treat for them.

She stepped back and peered into the highest limbs, her heart pinching painfully. "I cannot climb that tree. There is no way for me to get them down."

The nest balanced precariously on a flimsy-looking limb, in a "y"-shaped crook of the tree. It was not particularly well-built. It was a small miracle that the eggs had made it this long without the nest falling out of the tree.

Perhaps the fairy dragons who had built it were not particularly sensible creatures. Papa said sometimes those eggs were not worth saving as the hatchlings were too stupid to take care of themselves. Yes, it did seem rather cruel, but such was the way of things sometimes. Perhaps she should go back to the house and wait for him. She chewed her knuckle. Given that she was not even supposed to be in these woods in the first place, that might really be the best choice.

A roar of thunder shook the forest. But there were no clouds in the sky. Was that possible? A louder roar and the ground shook beneath her. She clutched her ears against the racket.

"Above!" Rumblkins ran circles around the tree.

She looked up and, by reflex alone, held out her apron as the nest tumbled out of the tree. With a small sideways jump, she caught the nest in the fabric, the eggs tumbling out and nearly rolling to the ground. Her foot slipped, and she landed solidly, jolting hard enough to cross her vision for a moment. Gracious! Her knees hurt, but the three leathery little eggs were safe!

Rumblkins wandered up beside her, sniffing and bumping her elbow with the top of his furry head. "I like eggs."

She gathered the apron around the eggs. "No, you may not have them. I have already promised you dried cod. You may not have these as well."

"Mrrow." He sounded only a little put out. If nothing else, the fish were definitely bigger than the eggs, so waiting would serve him well. Even he could see that.

Elizabeth placed the eggs back in the nest and removed her apron as more thunder roared. She wrapped the entire nest in her apron, tying the bundle securely. The ground shook so hard that she could barely get to her feet as leaves and small branches rained down upon her.

"Who is in my woods?" The voice was more of a roar than anything else.

Rumblkins ducked under her skirts, between her ankles, trembling.

"You know him?"

"That is Longbourn, and he is cranky. We have not been introduced, and I do not want to be."

"You are trespassing in my woods!" A large scaly head appeared out of the branches, long sharp teeth glistening in the sunlight.

So, that was what a wyvern looked like in person. Most of the illustrations in the Blue Order bestiaries were not entirely accurate. Most had the wings too small. Longbourn's wingspan was easily as wide as he was long, nose to tail tip, certainly broad enough to enable him to fly should he choose. His head was smaller than most illustrations depicted and more angular, not curved and elegant like a lizard's, but blocky and square. Glittery gold eyes sat wide on his face—probably so he could see around his rather large snout which sported intimidating fangs. He would have been somewhat frightening except for the long whiskers that hung down like a mustache from his snout, much like the one the parish vicar wore.

Nothing had prepared her for his smell, though. The little introduction Papa had given her was nothing to the real thing. Gracious, he stank—a mixture of musk, rotten meat, and bad teeth. Perhaps some tooth-powder and a bath would improve his scent. Surely it would not hurt. Should that not be the responsibility of the Dragon Keeper?

Longbourn leaned down and roared in her face, drops of spittle landing on her cheeks. "You are not supposed to be here. You have seen frightening shadows and will run home very frightened."

"No, I will not. You are not nearly so frightening as that." She stared into his eyes and crossed her arms.

Longbourn pulled back and sat on his haunches. "What did you say?"

"That you are quite rude trying to tell me what I should think when I can hear you quite well."

He squeezed his eyes shut and blinked several times. "It does not matter. You are in my territory and do not belong."

She tucked her apron under her arm and balanced her fists on her hips. "Yes, I do. I am daughter of your

Keeper and probably will be your Keeper myself in time. Who else belongs here more than me?" Granted, that all might be a bit of an exaggeration, but that was often a part of the dominance games dragons played.

Though there was no question that he was the dominant creature, she could still demand respect, and in so doing, earn his respect.

Longbourn pulled his head back and wrinkled his nose. He looked very funny doing so. He stepped forward, turning his head to and fro, studying her. "Keeper's daughter?"

"He never spoke of me?"

Longbourn snorted and stepped closer again. He leaned close and began smelling her, head to toes and back again. "You smell like him."

"There is good reason for that. I am his daughter. It is my right to be here."

"Why have you not been introduced to me?" He tapped the tip of his tail on the ground. Papa had a similar habit of tapping his foot when he was puzzled.

"For that, you must ask him. I have been very impatient for an introduction. So let me do it myself. I am Elizabeth Bennet. Soon, I hope to be Junior Keeper to Longbourn Keep." She curtsied deep enough to touch her knee to the ground and ducked her head.

Had she not been in line to be his Keeper, she would have touched her forehead to her ground and ideally wrapped her wings over her body and face to cover herself to accept his dominance—had she had wings. She really needed to finish making that cloak.

He scratched the dirt beside her, accepting her introduction. "You have taken something from me."

"No, I have not." She followed his gaze to her apron. "These are wild fairy dragon eggs. They are not yours."

"They are in my woods. They are mine." He shoved his nose at the apron under her arm.

She stepped back to avoid dropping them. Rude, pushy fellow. "Other dragons are not yours. They live in your woods, and you are their Laird. That is not the same as owning them."

"I have not given you permission to take them." He tried to nose her again.

She pushed back, and he stopped, eyes wide, even surprised. "I do not need your permission."

"Yes, you do." He stomped but not very hard.

"Not according to Papa and the Blue Order. They say it is our responsibility to save dragon lives whenever and wherever possible. That is what I am doing."

"Those are not dragons. They are eggs." He snuffed, splattering her with a bit of slimy stuff. Ugh!

What was he playing at? If he were truly upset, all this icky goo would contain enough of his venom that it would burn every place it touched her skin.

"Dragon eggs."

"Fairy dragons are worthless bits of fluff, hardly dragons at all." He rolled his eyes, much like Papa did.

"But they are dragons, nonetheless. I am going to take care of them, no matter what you say. You cannot bully me." She stood on tiptoes and glowered.

Longbourn's lip curled back, and he made the strangest sound. Was he laughing at her?

"I do not like being laughed at." She pulled back her shoulders and lifted her chin.

"Go home, Junior Keeper, and bring your father back with you to make a proper introduction. You just might do." Longbourn turned around, keeping his long tail carefully tucked in so as not to knock her off her feet, and wandered off back into the woods.

"You are very lucky he left so easily." Rumblkins peeked out from under her petticoat and pressed against her ankle. "He is very grouchy and smells bad. I want my fish now."

"Let us return to the house, and you shall have what I promised." Her knees trembled, and her hands shook as they walked back much more slowly than they had come. Had she really just met the estate dragon and been laughed at by him? How was she supposed to feel about that? And should she tell Papa what had happened?

Rumblkins enjoyed his prize with relish. Truly, it was not a pleasant thing to watch a dragon eat —especially a dragon devouring his very favorite food. But a promise was a promise, and he deserved his reward.

According to Mama, Papa was not expected until close to dinnertime, and Jane was in the nursery with her sisters, so she hurried up to her room with her carefully wrapped treasures, none the wiser for her adventures. She locked the door behind her and cleared her writing desk, moving the books from Papa's library and her writing supplies to the top of the press. Carefully, so very carefully, she placed her apron on the desk and unwrapped the nest.

It resembled a bird's nest, woven from twigs and vines, filled with thistle down and feathers gleaned from local chickens and ducks. Within were three eggs—according to the books, fairy dragons usually laid eggs in threes—about half the size of a chicken's egg, mottled and streaked, leathery rather than brittle.

With one finger, she stroked the eggs—they were just a mite soft, and she could feel small movements within. Little cheeps came from inside as she touched them.

She leaned down very close and whispered, "Are you there, little ones? Do you know I am here?"

The largest of the eggs wobbled just a little bit, as if in answer. Was that possible? Were the babies already able to hear and understand? That is not what she had been told about fairy dragons.

She retrieved her commonplace book from the shelf and found the notes she had made from Papa's Dragon Bestiary. No, she remembered correctly. Other sorts of eggs responded to the human voice, especially very near hatching, but there was no record of fairy dragons doing so. Definitely something to make note of. Once she finished recording those details, she sketched the nest and the eggs themselves, including her hairbrush in the drawing to offer some scale. Far more interesting than the still life Mama suggested she try to sketch recently.

No, she was not the best at sketching yet, but even Mama would suggest this was good practice for her, if, a mite unusual. It certainly was not an opportunity to waste. When would she get another opportunity to see dragon eggs?

Hatchings did not happen every day, and to be entirely honest with herself, she was very low on the scale of who might be expected to have the opportunity to befriend a dragon, no matter how much she might wish for it. A little girl of a country gentleman's house just did not rate that sort of favor, even for a mere fairy dragon. Not to mention, Papa adamantly opposed having a house dragon. So she needed to make the most of this opportunity.

A knock at the door made her jump. Had it already gotten so late? When had the sun sunk so low in the sky?

"Lizzy? Let me in." Papa's voice sounded just a touch irritated.

She hurried to unlock the door.

"What have you been about that you have been looking for me and yet left the door locked?" He stepped in, closing the door behind him.

She edged in front of the writing desk. "It has all been so very urgent this morning. Yet you were not home. I tried to find you, very diligently, really I did. But at last I had to do the best I could on my own."

His brows knotted as he looked at her. His gaze drifted to the desk behind her. "What is that?"

She looked over her shoulder. "That is the urgent business I was talking about."

"That is not urgent business; it is a fairy dragon nest. What is it doing here?" He rolled his eyes the way he did when he was exasperated with Mama.

"Rumblkins found me this morning and told me that the brood parents had abandoned it to sleep through the cold season and there was a stoat endangering the eggs." She grabbed his hand and pulled him toward her writing desk.

He dragged his hand over his face.

"Rumblkins took me to them and the nest fell out of the tree—in a gust of wind—" So that bit was not true, but he looked so very annoyed right now, trying to tell him that Longbourn had been involved seemed like a very bad idea. "And I caught it in my apron as it fell."

"Of course it did." His lips pulled tight in something not quite a grimace but definitely not a smile. "It just fell into your lap with no assistance from the tatzelwurm?"

"He did nothing to the nest, Papa. Absolutely nothing." At least that part was entirely true. "And he was right, there were stoat tracks all around the tree. Had I waited, the eggs would no doubt have been eaten."

He sank into the little white chair beside the desk, forehead in his hand.

She clutched her skirts, crushing them in her hands, the way Mama always told her not to. "We rescued the eggs, Papa. That is a good thing, is it not? That is what the Blue Order says we are to do—protect and preserve dragon life whenever we are able. And I did that today, did I not?"

"Oh, Lizzy." He sighed and rubbed his tired blue eyes. "Yes, I suppose that is the case."

"You do not seem pleased, Papa." She swallowed hard and bit her lips.

"Perhaps not. It is complicated, my dear." He raked his hair back.

"I do not understand." Her heart thundered, threatening to lodge in her throat.

He ran his fingers over the edge of the nest. "Fairy dragons are, well, they are barely dragons in many ways. They are on the verge of being nuisances to man and dragon alike."

"They are small and cute and sometimes not very smart—that makes them nuisances?" The same thing could be said of Lydia and Kitty, but no one called them nuisances, at least not in Elizabeth's hearing.

"There is a reason they are considered well—useless little flutterbobs and flitterbits. They have no territory, no wisdom to impart. They are not particularly useful and not even very good company."

"Does that mean they are not important? They are dragons after all." She gripped her hands tightly together.

"Yes, they are dragons, but, how can I explain? They reproduce at a much faster rate than other dragons so there are many, many nests." He pinched his temples with thumb and forefinger.

"But they are also eaten by other creatures at a much higher rate. How many other dragons are preyed upon by stoats, cats, and birds of prey, not to mention nearly every other dragon type?"

He shook his head, not looking up. "That is what it means to be the least of the dragons. If their numbers were not kept in check, we would be overrun with them."

"They do not breed that fast." She huffed a little but caught herself before Papa could react.

"You do not know that. Trust me, it would be a problem."

"So I was wrong to save the nest?" She sniffled a little, her eyes burning.

"Had I been here, I would have counseled you that we ought to allow nature to take its course and permit things to happen as they ordinarily would."

How could she have possibly been expected to neglect these wee little things who were already cheeping and recognizing her presence? "What will you do with them now?" She held her breath and forced herself to stand very still.

Papa carefully examined the eggs, holding them up to his ears, eyes closed. He stroked them firmly, holding his thumb over them, twitching slightly as each egg responded. With a distinct harrumph, he returned them to the nest. "They are very close to hatching. It does not bode well that the brood parents would mate too late in the season for the eggs to hatch in summer, though. They are likely to be especially stupid creatures."

She nodded, staring at the blurry floorboards.

"But it will not do to waste the opportunity, I suppose. There are always those among the Order who are desirous of companions for wives and daughters who hear. I will make inquiries and if there are potential Friends near, then I will make arrangements." He pushed himself up from the chair, grunting.

And if not? The question danced on the tip of her tongue, but perhaps it was best not to ask. Contenting herself with this much good news was probably for the best right now.

4
Chapter

!

The eggs spent the night in her room. With no proper nesting box, it was as good a place as any, according to Papa. That it also gave her a little more time to spend with them was a happy coincidence.

He assured her that the eggs did not need to be kept any warmer than her room, else she might have tucked them into her bed with her. He probably knew that. Still, she wrapped the nest in her apron and moved her writing desk a little closer to the fireplace when a cold rain began falling outside. No sense in taking any chances. Her little guests should be as comfortable as she could make them.

She fell asleep staring at the wrapped nest and slept more soundly than she had in a very long time. Could the little egg-bound dragons have been singing her to sleep, thanking her for a warm, safe place to weather the evening's storm? Papa would declare her fanciful and silly, but it was definitely possible.

At the very least, it would not hurt to record it in her commonplace book. It was the sort of thing one wished to remember. She carefully edged her commonplace book next to the nest and recorded her observations before making her way down to the morning room.

After breakfast, Papa called her to his office and asked that she bring her "bundle" with her. What would Mama think to know they had dragon eggs in the house? Probably best not to find out. Still, even if she told Mama directly, Mama would probably only laugh at her, pat her on the head, and scold Papa for encouraging too much imagination in her. That was what Mama usually said when the subject of dragons came up. Not that it did very often, but perhaps a little more often than it might in a non-dragon-keeping household.

She sighed as she trekked upstairs. What would it be like to live in a place where one could freely discuss dragons and all things related to them, one where dragons were welcome and walked the corridors as freely as the people? She had never been in such a place, but surely they must exist, mustn't they?

A low fire glowed in the fireplace of Papa's study, warming the room just a mite. Sometimes he did that because his joints hurt. But today, given that he had cleared a wider than usual path through the chaos, as well as space for a wooden box filled with hay near the hearth, it seemed it was more for the eggs.

Even though she was accustomed to it by now, it still struck her how, for being such a very particular man, Papa's study was a picture of refined disorder. Somewhere in the piles, the ledgers for the household must be hiding, but they were probably near the bottom of a stack given the way Mama complained about his lack of attention to the estate accounts this morning.

The chess table near the window held several mahogany dragons carved in precise detail along with the chess pieces. A white dragon and a black dragon, one for each side of the board. One could almost imagine fierce dragons attacking and devouring a medieval army. Papa once said the wooden dragons were exact models of an amphithere and a lindwurm. They were among his most treasured possessions.

An heirloom dragon perch, resembling a dining room chair without a seat, stood between a pair of comfortable arm chairs. Uncle Gardiner's Friend cockatrice, Rustle, perched there when he visited. How odd that Mama's brother could hear dragons but she could not. Last time he had visited, he had asked Papa's advice about becoming betrothed to a woman who could not hear dragons. Papa had little good to say about the practice—directly in front of Elizabeth. Apparently he had forgotten she was in the room writing letters for him when that conversation took place. How strenuously he had warned her not to say anything of the discussion to anyone, especially Mama.

The floor was strewn with towers of books nearly as high as her waist. He often muttered that he really needed to get them all back on the shelves, but it did not take a grown man to see that there was no possible way all his books would fit on the study shelves. He would need at least another room of shelves to accomplish that. She wove her way around them into the room.

He locked the door behind them, not that anyone

was really likely to disturb them. No one liked to bother Papa when he was ensconced in his book room. For good reason.

"Take the eggs to the nesting box, there." He pointed toward the hearth with his chin and shambled behind her.

The rough wooden box had been fashioned of weathered, gray boards that had clearly seen some past use outside. The box came halfway up her shins and had been sanded more or less smooth. The sides were a bit uneven—most likely something one of the grooms had cobbled together, not the work of a proper carpenter. But that was not something little dragons would notice or care about. Clean, sweet-smelling hay filled the interior about two thirds of the way to the top. Propped up against the hearth was what must be a lid for the box and a small coil of rope to tie it on with.

Was it wrong to be just a little sad, knowing that the little dragons were going away and she would not get to see them after they hatched? Probably, but those thoughts needed to be kept to herself. Especially since they were going to a place where Friends would keep them safe from the abundant dangers to fairy dragons.

"Put the whole nest in the center of the hay. Dig out a little well for it first and lay them gently inside." Papa gestured with his hands.

She unwrapped her apron and nestled her burden into the box. If she closed her eyes, she could just barely hear soft, sweet cheeping. She yawned.

"That is how you know for certain these are fairy dragon eggs. Tatzelwurm eggs look very similar, but their eggs are laid in burrows, not in trees, and the eggs, well, they sort of purr—that is the best description of the sound—whilst these will set you to sleeping as quickly as full-grown fairy dragons."

That was something she would need to write down in her commonplace book.

Papa hunkered down beside her and removed the largest egg from the nest. He held it up in the sunlight, turned it around in his hands, and tapped on the shell. "They are not far from hatching. A se'nnight, maybe ten days at the most. You can tell by the sound they make and the condition of the shell. Come, look."

She pressed in close, her shoulder touching his. He smelt like herbal liniment and willow bark tea.

"You see how it feels like tough shoe leather, but just a bit malleable? As it gets closer to hatching, it becomes more like a supple boot rather than the hard sole. And you can feel the chick inside tapping back against your finger. When you can feel the sharp tip of the beak, then hatching is only a day or so day away."

"You are not quite there yet, are you?" She whispered to the egg in her hands.

"Did you know, several tomes of dragon lore say that it is good to speak to eggs before they hatch, that it assists the chicks in imprinting since they already know the sound of human voices?" He smiled that rare approving smile that made her feel all warm and furry inside.

"Might that be my job then while we wait for them to hatch?"

He smiled as though he had intended for her to ask just that. "I have another job for you, first. Perhaps you might talk to them when you are finished."

She clasped her hands tightly and tried not to fidget—he always warned her not to do that. "What may I do?"

"I know of several Blue Order families within a day's journey from Longbourn who might be in want of a Dragon Friend for the ladies of the household."

"No boys?"

"Few consider fairy dragons a manly companion, so usually they are relegated to the ladies."

Elizabeth chewed her lip. Any more questions would probably make Papa cross.

"I will dictate the first letter to you. After that, you can copy it over several times, substituting in the proper names and details to each. I must get those out in today's post. There is no time to waste in finding proper homes for these eggs." He reached behind him to push against a chair to help him rise. His knees were probably bothering him again.

"What will happen if we cannot?" She held her breath.

Papa sighed. "We will take them out to the barn and let them hatch there with us in attendance, of course. It does not hurt to have them properly imprinted upon humans, but there is no need to have them living in the house with us. Your mother would hardly accept them."

She nodded, still holding her breath. At least the little dragons would hatch safely. Perhaps she could convince Rumblkins to watch after them until they were big enough to fly. That way, the barn cats and tatzelwurms might not interfere with them. They might even choose to live in the barn and help keep down some of the flies. She might even visit them occasionally that way.

Even so, it would have been much nicer if they could have lived in the house.

Several days later, Papa trundled into his study bearing several thick letters from the day's post. She had tried to tidy the study, but her successes were difficult to see. All the surfaces had been thoroughly dusted—what a task that had been! When was the last time the maid had been permitted in the room? It still smelt of dust and old books, but a little less of dust than it had before.

At least there was a good reason for all his clutter—dragon lore had to be preserved for posterity—though Mama would simply insist he had too many books and should get rid of them. It was probably impolitic to say so, but he would probably sooner get rid of Mama than his books.

Elizabeth sat beside the nesting box, reading to the eggs from *Dragon Etiquette Volume 1: Greetings,* her throat decidedly raw and scratchy. Maintaining a steady stream of conversation toward the eggs proved more challenging than she had expected. Apparently, she lacked her mother and Aunt Philips' ability to talk endlessly over all matter of idle nothings. She had run out of things to say halfway through the day before in the midst of dusting.

But Papa said it was good for the eggs to be spoken to, so reading to them seemed a reasonable compromise. He came in just after she had opened the book and started reading, giving her that special look for when he knew she was beyond reasoning with and shaking his head. But he let her remain with the eggs, which was what she really wanted, so all was well enough.

Papa wove his way through the forest of furniture

and piles and settled into his favorite wingchair on the opposite side of the nesting box. He laid a stack of correspondence in his lap and thumbed through them.

"Are any of those responses to the letters you sent?" Elizabeth set the heavy book aside and balanced her elbows on her knees, hands clasped tightly.

"It seems so." Three of the letters bore the blue sealing wax used by the Order, but he set those aside. "I will attend to business first, though." He used his voice that was not to be argued with.

She swallowed back a sigh. How many times had Mama told her she must learn patience? No sense in wasting the opportunity. At least that is what Mama, and probably Jane, would say.

Elizabeth returned to reading to the eggs. Probably just as well. She was on the section about wyverns, and since Longbourn was a wyvern, it behooved her to be thoroughly versed in their forms of etiquette, especially what one did with one's wings. That seemed vitally important. Since fairy dragons also had wings, this could be pertinent to them, too—if they could understand, which Papa was certain they did not.

Regardless of the fairy dragons' ability to understand, the instructions were incredibly interesting. Even though on the surface, it all read as a very dull list of dos and do nots—tedious to remember and painfully detailed—she had recently discovered it was far more thought-provoking than that.

Read on the whole, patterns became evident, both within the species and between them. When one teased those out, the behaviors and rituals actually began to make sense and were not that difficult to remember. Threats, like fangs and claws, were exposed by the dominant dragon, covered or hidden by the submitting one who kept their head lower than the dominant's. The specifics of just how that was done, though, took a great many pages to explain.

Papa grunted and muttered under his breath. "Well, that is a disappointment. It seems Corthwallis has no interest in fairy dragons. His daughter has got herself betrothed and does not need the distraction right now. Staines' daughter found herself a tatzelwurm to befriend—and I do not envy him that; they are such addle-pates—and does not think it wise to have a little fairy dragon in the house with a young, and likely still ill-mannered, tatzelwurm. I must agree. It is not a good thing for members of the same household to eat one another, no matter how much a course of nature it might be. I discourage it wholeheartedly." Papa set aside that letter and chuckled at his own joke.

But really, all things considered, it was hardly that humorous.

It was difficult to know how to feel. On the one hand, it was sad that no one seemed to want to befriend these little eggs. On the other, it would be nice to have them close to Longbourn, if, of course, she could keep the chicks safe …

Papa cracked the seal on another letter and flicked at the stiff paper. "Oh, yes, these are much better tidings from Baronet Delves. Old Rowley was a school mate of mine, you know. He lives in Oakforde, twenty or so miles north of Meryton on an estate called Pembroke. He has three daughters and a son, all of whom can hear. The girls, he says, are wild for fairy dragons and would gladly befriend our little clutch."

"That is good then, is it not?" She bit her lip, forcing her voice to stay light and pleasing.

"All in all, I would have to say it is. The girls are a

bit silly themselves, but that should not be a problem. Fairy dragons are not known for being very particular in their choice of Friends." Papa set the letter aside and resettled himself in his chair.

Perhaps they would be more particular if they had a better choice of Friends. If only silly, inconsequential people were encouraged to be interested in befriending them, of course fairy dragons would seem flighty and mindless. No one would think fairy dragons worthless if the King had one as a Friend.

What an absurd idea, the King of England with a fairy dragon perched on his crown, joining him on official events. She giggled under her breath.

"So, get your writing things out and help me draft a letter to Delves. We shall leave for Pembroke the day after tomorrow." He pointed toward the little table that she used as a writing desk in the corner by the window. Naturally, he had covered the entire surface with papers and open journals.

"We, Papa?" Could she have heard that correctly? Just in case she did, she sat very still and very straight lest he deny he had said it.

"Yes, I intend to bring you with me. You are proving yourself a good observer. It will be good practice for you to hone your skills of observation. We may discuss your findings on the way home. There is something to be learned from all hatchings, even very insignificant ones like this one. Moreover, the details of the hatching should be recorded. For that, I need your hands. I mean to begin on the dragon hatchings book that I have been intending to write after we return."

"Am I to help you with that project, too?" She bit her lip and held her breath. Pray let him say yes! What could possibly be better than helping him pen his book and talk to him about it in the process? What better way to learn about hatchings than from the man who had attended more than any other currently alive in the Order?

"Yes. I thought about hiring a secretary from the Order to do the job, but I cannot justify the expense this year. The weather has not been favorable, and the crops have not been as fruitful as I had anticipated." He leaned back, lifted his glasses, and rubbed his eyes.

Mama had hinted about some tightness in the budget when she had talked about new gowns for Jane since she had grown too tall for her current ones.

"I am afraid you are young for the task, but there is nothing to be done for that. We must not allow it to become well-known that you have assisted me, though, lest the work is looked down upon for your participation. I know you are an accurate scribe, but not everyone will attribute that skill to you."

Perhaps she should be offended at his concern over how she might "contaminate" the reputation of his work. But the promise of learning so much that others did not know was more than sufficient to make up for it. "I will not disappoint you, Papa. I shall write it very well for you."

"I know you will, my dear, but now, the letter to Delves."

For the journey to Oakforde, Papa presented her with *Dragon Etiquette Vol 2: Conversations.* She balanced it on her lap with one hand and steadied the box next to her with the other, occasionally clutching both tightly as the old carriage swayed along the rough road.

Mama complained the carriage should be re-sprung, but somehow, it did not seem very likely.

Although the tome's initial illustrations promised a fascinating read, it did not prove nearly so gripping as the volume on greetings. The entire text could be summed up in: Do not speak first, do not disagree, do not offer topics of conversation interesting to humans and—just in case she did not remember from the first time it had been said— do not disagree. Of course, all the strictures applied primarily to major dragons and those larger minor dragons who might think they rivaled a human for dominance and who might prove injurious should they be provoked.

But what kind of basis of a friendly relationship could that provide? Really, it sounded like the way one might talk to a king, not to a friend. She would never have shared all those lovely conversations with Rumblkins under those rules. Then again, he was a very minor dragon among minor dragons and did not expect anyone to care about his opinions. He was quite happy to find someone interested in what he thought and liked—even if it was mostly dried cod and warm milk—and he did not mind differing opinions at all.

Did Papa actually support all those rules, or was this just one of those books that one read because they had to, then promptly forgot in favor of more practical approaches? There were a few of those among his collection, not that he came out precisely and called them that. It was clear, though, there were some he respected less than others.

She shoved the book into her carpetbag and began talking to the eggs again, very softly, so as not to disturb Papa.

Several hours later, including the stop to rest the horses, Pembroke rose on the horizon—a magnificent house on very pleasing grounds at least twice the size of Longbourn, maybe more. The design was very modern—like something out of one of Mama's magazines—the sort of style in which she wanted Papa to rebuild Longbourn. Light and bright, it was easy to see why Mama liked it so. But there was nothing wrong with Longbourn as it was, so rebuilding was unlikely to happen whilst Papa was master there. He disliked unnecessary changes.

The woods resembled those at Longbourn, with many tall hardwoods and rocky hillsides that probably contained a dragon lair. Papa called these sorts of copses "dragon woods" because so many dragon lairs were established in such places.

Perhaps there were wild fairy dragons here, too. At the very least, it appeared the sort of place that fairy dragons would like to live. Good, her little friends had an excellent chance of being happy here. Next to being happy at Longbourn, it was the best possible thing.

The driver stopped the carriage at Pembroke's imposing front door. Oak bound with iron, it looked more medieval than modern. It must have been some sort of family heirloom as the image of a rather grumpy basilisk was carved into it. Rough and Gothic, the carving only made the poor dragon look crankier—the sort one would not want to accidentally meet on a dark night—or maybe even in the bright daylight.

A somber and somewhat cranky-looking butler led them inside the manor and to what appeared to be the master's office. Their driver trundled behind with the nesting box. Elizabeth would much rather have carried it herself, but it would not have been proper.

The office was bright and spacious with doors that enclosed the bookshelves and kept all the volumes neatly contained. A small stack of papers occupied one corner of the desk, but it was neatly arranged and held in place with a paperweight bearing the seal of the Blue Order. If he actually did any work in this room, he just was as different from Papa as a firedrake was to a major wyrm.

"Rowley, old chum, how are you?" Papa extended his hand toward a very proper, not at all cranky-looking gentleman.

Sir Rowley, Baronet Delves, stood head and shoulders taller than Papa. He was very thin, so much so that a mere breeze might blow him away. His movements were a mite awkward, all elbows and knees, but his toothy smile seemed genuine, and his dark eyes were kind. "So kind of you to drag yourself all the way out to Oakforde on behalf of my daughters."

"I suppose men with many daughters must indeed stick together, no?" Papa shrugged a bit. "May I present Elizabeth, my second daughter."

Elizabeth curtsied as Mama had taught her.

"Elizabeth has read a great deal on fairy dragons and observed even more of their nature in the Longbourn woods. She will be able to instruct your girls on what to expect during the hatching and how they are to care for the hatchlings afterward."

Sir Rowley nodded at her. "I am pleased to meet you. My daughters will be here in just a moment. They will be very glad to meet you. I have told them you will be teaching them about fairy dragons. They are at that age where they do not like to be instructed by their father. I think they would listen to you a great deal more readily than they would to me."

The study door swung open a little farther, and three young ladies, all in white muslin dresses with different color ribbons, appeared. They were all tall and slim like their father, but more willowy than gangly. The eldest looked near maybe seventeen or eighteen and definitely out in society, the youngest probably close to fifteen. They shared similar features but were hardly identical. The youngest was by far the prettiest, the eldest plain by comparison, though she probably did not like hearing that. They did not look like the sort of girls who would much appreciate listening to someone younger than themselves, though.

"May I present my daughters, Emily, Elaine, and Eva." He gestured toward them in turn. "My son is out right now, but he will be joining us for dinner tonight."

Chances were his name was Edmond or Edward or Ezra. Elizabeth sneaked a glance at Papa. He had a funny little pet peeve about naming one's children all starting with the same first letter. He thought it showed an alarming lack of creativity in a parent.

"We are pleased to meet you," the girls said in unison and curtsied together as though it were something they practiced. Though their expressions were mild enough, something about their dark eyes was not entirely comforting.

"Girls, take Miss Bennet for some refreshments. She can tell you a very great deal about the little dragons that are going to be joining our household."

"Yes, Papa." Miss Delves beckoned her toward the door and led the parade to a small parlor near the back of the house. Although they walked very quickly, Elizabeth was left with the impression of a house that was very bright, airy, and full of black and white marble. "The maid will bring some refreshments shortly."

Fine, modern furniture filled the parlor—obviously, it had recently been redone. Many paintings, mostly portraits, lined the white walls. Crisp dark red drapes flanked the tall windows that looked out onto the garden. Finer than any room at Longbourn, it was tasteful and elegant, perhaps even a bit understated. Not at all to Mama's taste, but Elizabeth found it quite comfortable.

Miss Elaine and Miss Eva sat on opposite sides of a small, round table inlaid with a scene depicting the establishment of the Pendragon Accords, and stared at Elizabeth.

"I understand you are from a small estate near Meryton," Miss Delves seated herself between her sisters and folded her hands in her lap. Was that a bit of derision in her voice? "Do you get many travelers there from London?"

Elizabeth settled herself on the remaining chair, an ugly duckling amongst the swans. "Yes, we are but three hours from London. Sometimes it seems there is a steady stream to and from there."

"Papa said I am to have a season in London soon as I have just come out." Miss Delves squared her shoulders and lifted her chin in a very superior sort of way.

No wonder she would feel that way, for a girl who was out could hardly be expected to converse with a mere child like Elizabeth.

Even if that child had important information for her. But that was probably an ungenerous thought.

"He promised that for all of us in our turns," Miss Elaine's voice contained a rather envious note.

"It is the best place to find husbands, after all." The look in Miss Eva's eye suggested she hoped to be adding something new to the conversation.

"So you are very interested in husbands and beaux?" Elizabeth traced the imagery on the table with her fingertip. The artist had gotten part of the scene wrong—

"Of course! I understand how you might not yet be; you are so young, after all. But really, what else is there worth being interested in?" Miss Delves laughed, shrill and thin, as though she were trying to prove something.

The maid brought in a pitcher of lemonade and a generous platter of sandwiches and biscuits which Miss Delves quickly served. Elizabeth tried not to lick her lips.

"I find dragons very interesting." Elizabeth nibbled the edge of a sandwich stuffed with ham and some sort of sharp cheese. "Your father and mine said I should tell you about fairy dragons."

"They are small, colorful, and they sing prettily. What more need one know?" Miss Elaine tossed her head and rolled her eyes, mimicking her elder sister's attitude.

"Well, to start with, I suppose, they have many names. They are also called fly-dragons, humming dragons, European hai-riyo, Lesser hai-riyo." Elizabeth kept her eyes on her plate. It was unlikely they should be as interested in such things as she was.

"Fly-dragons! Humming dragons? How very silly." Miss Eva giggled behind her hand.

Miss Delves shared a conspiratorial look with Miss Eva. "They are also referred to as flutterbobs, flufflebits, fluttertufts, flitter-jibbits, and ear-nips. At least according to our brother."

"Papa says that they are not generally the sort of

companion a man is likely to have, so it would not be surprising he does not have a great deal of respect for them. They are, after all, the smallest known of dragon species. The largest is no larger than a man's hand; usually, they are the size of a small songbird or hummingbird. Usually, the dragon deaf are persuaded to believe them to be hummingbirds."

"Does it not seem odd to you that they would persuade people to believe they are a species that is not even native to Britain?" How smug Miss Delves looked.

"But hummingbirds are known here."

"By prints and pictures and the like. If they were a little more intelligent, I think they would have persuaded non-hearers to think they were simply different sorts of songbirds." Miss Delves nodded at her sisters.

"I suppose, but if one is observant, they could see that a fairy dragon is different to a bird. While they have a birdlike body, wings, and legs, their tails can be bird-like or more dragon-like, a little like a cockatrice with its serpentine lower half. Their heads are distinctly draconic, and their beaks have sharp teeth. By choosing something exotic to conceal themselves as, they facilitate their persuasions being accepted."

Miss Elaine's lip curled back just a mite. It was not an attractive expression on her. "So then they are not very good at persuasions?"

Patience. Mama said she needed to learn patience. She should be grateful for another opportunity. "I am told they are among the most persuasive of dragons—only just a little less than tatzelwurms—but there are limits even for them. It is nearly impossible to persuade someone away from something they are very determined to believe."

"They are very pretty creatures, though. The ones that live in the woods here are mostly green and blue." Miss Eva looked over her shoulder toward the garden windows.

"They can also be red and purple. The male who sired this clutch is a very lovely lavender and purple. He is very easy to see when he visits the garden. Unfortunately, that makes it difficult to conceal themselves from predators."

Miss Eva gasped, wide-eyed. "Predators? They are dragons! Nothing eats dragons."

"Pray forgive me for disagreeing with you, but that is hardly the case. Large dragons eat smaller dragons in the wild. All sorts of wyrms and cockatrice, even drakes will snack on fairy dragons when they can. Cats and rats, stoats, dogs and foxes, they will all eat them as well."

"How horrid!" Miss Elaine pressed her hand to her chest.

"Papa says it is necessary to keep the population in check. But I do not like to think about it." Elizabeth shuddered just a bit. "I imagine that you will need to keep your Friends protected against a very dangerous world."

Miss Delves caught her lower lip in her teeth. "I had no idea the creature would demand so much from us. Will we need to feed them, too, or do they feed themselves?"

"Bedlow, the baby drake I know, is fed by his Friend, but he is far too young to be able to find his own food just yet. So I imagine at least while they are young, you will need to provide their victuals."

"What do they eat?" Miss Eva asked.

"They catch bugs, you ninny!" Miss Elaine sneered.

"Do you not recall seeing them chasing dragonflies and May beetles?"

"Ewww, how horrid. I do not care what you say, I am not—"

"I have it on good authority that not all of them eat bugs. They are the only dragons known for liking sweets. The pair that provided this clutch is very fond of them. Sometimes, I bring a dish of jam or a saucer of honey to the garden for them. They are very happy for it and sing very sweetly to me when I do it."

"Jam and honey are much pleasanter than creepy bugs." Miss Eva settled back in her seat.

"Even if they are of the type that prefers insects, I am told that they can be satisfied with bits of sausage, forced meat, even puddings. Certainly your father will see to the dragons' comfort as well as your own."

"Dragons." Miss Elaine rolled her eyes. "Everything is dragons with Father. Everything."

"That is the only thing he will talk to us about. Dragons and how important it is to manage the needs of an estate dragon." Miss Eva's lip curled as though she were drinking sour milk.

"Have you met your estate dragon yet?" Elizabeth sipped her too-sour lemonade.

Miss Delves shared a knowing look with her sisters. "Hardly. Pembroke is a very crusty, cranky, cantankerous soul, we are told. He likes no one and sees no one but Papa, and him only when it is absolutely necessary. He is a basilisk, you know, and they are the most unfriendly creatures. But it really is not a bad thing. He puts very few demands on any of us, so dragon keeping is hardly a burden at all."

"Do you not find it disappointing not to be able to meet him and interact, though? Basilisks live even longer than firedrakes. The stories he must have to tell!" Oh, the looks they gave her! As though they thought her daft.

"As if he would lower himself to storytelling to anyone, much less any of us!" Miss Elaine snickered.

Miss Eva peered at her through narrow eyes. "You are a very silly, very peculiar girl, I do say."

So that was how it was to be. Ah well, it was not too far different from dealing with Mama—except that she could openly talk about dragons. "Perhaps I should confine my conversation to the nature of fairy dragons as your father suggested."

"They are such pretty colorful little things I should think having one as a Friend would help attract the attention of eligible young dragon keepers." Miss Delves suddenly appeared interested. "Have you anything else to tell us of them?"

"Pray enough now, it is all so dreadful dull." Miss Elaine's eyes opened wide, and she smiled. But somehow it did not look very trustworthy. Odd how it was more difficult to tell with human expressions than dragon ones. "I have a better idea. Let us show you what we mean about Pembroke, and you will think he is as dreadful as we do."

"I cannot imagine that."

"Come then, and we will show you." Miss Elaine beckoned them all out the garden door.

"No, I am not going. I hate that part of the woods, and you cannot make me go." Miss Eva crossed her arms and stomped.

"Fine, be a baby! Go upstairs to the nursery then. We will go to the woods." Miss Elaine tossed her head and marched out.

Elizabeth hesitated and bit her lip. Perhaps she

should remain behind, too. But she was supposed to teach the girls about fairy dragons. She could not do that if she did not stay with them. And it would be very interesting to see where a basilisk lived, perhaps even catch a glimpse of the creature as well.

5
Chapter

Miss Delves took a path through the flower garden, which was much like the one at Longbourn, but much larger and better maintained. Michaelmas daisies, sunflowers, and coneflowers, some taller than she, swayed in the breeze, perfuming the air with sweetness that attracted bees, birds, butterflies, and the tiniest of dragons.

"This is the sort of place that fairy dragons would like very much. When the chicks are older, I am sure they will enjoy coming out here to feed."

"Feeding them cannot be so difficult, I am sure. I will take mine out here as soon as it hatches." Miss Elaine snorted.

"But even in the wild, parents feed the newly-hatched, at least until they can fly." Elizabeth pushed several drooping stems out of her way.

"Those are the sorts of chores the servants do."

Miss Elaine glared at Elizabeth over her shoulder and walked faster.

Elizabeth ran to keep up. Should she tell Papa these might not be the sort of girls who should keep dragons?

Miss Delves pointed toward the woods that bordered the garden. "There, Pembroke lives in there."

The woods resembled those that were home to Longbourn's lair, old hardwoods creating deep shade. These were more dense than what Longbourn preferred, though. Was it because a basilisk tended to be lower to the ground and better able to navigate tighter confines? A wyvern, with his height and substantial wings, seemed like he would require far more space in which to move around.

Miss Elaine grabbed her hand and pulled her ahead of Miss Delves. "You see there, that hill in the distance? You can just make it out. That is the dragon's lair."

"Is that all? I had expected something rather more imposing for a basilisk. It looks like a very regular sort of hill that houses a dragon cave. Hardly the sort of place to become worked up about." Elizabeth shrugged.

The Miss Delveses—or should that have been the Misses Delves or the Misses Delveses?—Jane would probably know—seemed disappointed.

Miss Elaine planted her fists on her hips and cocked her head. "There is a stream that runs through the woods, too. One that has all sorts of water dragons—"

"Wyrms? Or does a small knucker live there? They are said to be very mischievous. Basilisks are quite serious, though. I cannot see the one living so near the lair of the other. Dragons, especially large ones, tend to be very solitary." At least according to dragon lore, they were.

"You certainly seem to know everything there is to know about dragons." Miss Delves tossed her head and rolled her eyes. Jane sometimes did that when she found Elizabeth exasperating.

"Certainly not. I have only read a very few of my father's books on dragons. Though I took a great many notes, I cannot imagine that I remember even half of what I read. There are so many things to learn about dragons."

Miss Delves slapped her forehead. "I bet you like dragons better than you do boys."

"Have you ever even thought about a boy?" Miss Elaine leaned very close to her face.

"I have thought about Dragon Keepers." Why would she even give a thought to anyone else?

"See, I told you. She is some sort of dragon bluestocking." Miss Elaine sniffed at her sister then turned back to Elizabeth. "Such an odd little thing. I do not know if I like you very well at all."

"I suppose it is good then that we live so far apart. You are in very little way of seeing me after Papa and I go home." Poor little fairy dragons. Such dreadful girls to be their Friends. "I should like to return to the house now."

"After we have come this far? Hardly. Come, we are nearly at the stream that runs alongside of the lair." Miss Delves caught her hand and pulled her along into the dark woods.

The little stream, deep enough for small fish and perhaps a few water wyrms, babbled a greeting to them. Rocky, muddy banks lined each side, damp, but probably not too slippery. Certainly it was not large enough for a knucker to live there, which was just as well as she had read very little about them.

Wyrms, though, she was very comfortable with and welcomed a conversation with them. They could probably tell her a great deal about Pembroke. It would be lovely to hear some firsthand observations of a basilisk.

"Follow the stream. It will lead to the lair." Miss Elaine gave her a little push. "We are right behind you."

As it seemed the only way to get them to take her back to the house, she pushed on. Long, slithery wyrm tracks followed the edge of the water on the other side of the stream. Was that a forest wyrm that hunted fish, or a water wyrm looking for a sliver of sunbeam to bask in? She would have to try and remember its shape and sketch it tonight. Then she might be able to compare it to the pictures in the dragon bestiary in Papa's office.

Overhanging branches screened out most of the sunlight. One might see these woods as dark and imposing, if one were not accustomed to such places. Perhaps that was the Miss Delveses' problem —they did not come here often enough to understand the beauty of the place. Maybe if she helped them see—

She glanced over her shoulder. Where were they? No, certainly they could not be that horrid. "Miss Elaine? Miss Delves? I do not know the way back! You must take me back to the house!"

Silence. Deep silence. The sort of silence that was not natural for the forest.

"Run, little girl. You do not belong here. You are trespassing on my territory. Run away in terror and never return." The voice was low and resounding, almost melodious, in a terrifying sort of way. "You are very, very afraid."

A little chill ran down her spine. He was very good at persuasion to be able to accomplish that. If he treated the Miss Delveses that way, no wonder they were not fond of him.

She turned and locked eyes with a great, shadowy basilisk. There was a reason legends said its gaze would kill. The fabulous animal was utterly terrifying—or at least would be to one who did not expect its presence. Easily twelve feet long, its snake-like body rose up on four lizardly legs. Mottled black and brown, it blended in with the forest floor. The serpentine head bore a yellow-gold crest of spiky feather-scales that resembled nothing so much as a crown, making him very regal, indeed.

The fangs, long enough to be seen even when his mouth was closed, were off-putting. One glittered with what must be a drop of venom. Probably part of his show to scare away trespassers.

But, she knew what most trespassers would not. The Blue Order forbade him from harming humans, unless he was directly threatened. And a young unarmed girl, all alone, was hardly a genuine threat. So, fear was the only weapon he could turn on her. And knowing that, she was hardly afraid.

"Pray forgive my trespass, sir." She dropped to the ground, pulling her shawl up over her head and extending her arms and legs, making herself as long and low to the ground as possible. It was difficult making her head lower than his.

The ground was damp and smelt musky and pleasant and would probably stain her skirt. But, it was best to follow the book's advice on greetings, making herself appear as small, harmless, and low as she could before the more powerful beast.

She really did need to finish that cloak. It would be so much easier to cover properly with that.

"You hear?" Pembroke circled her, sniffing her thoroughly.

"I am daughter of Keeper Bennet of Longbourn. We are the invited guests of Sir Rowley," she muttered into the ground. It seemed a rather silly way to have a conversation, but he might become offended if she rose too soon.

"You bring the fairy dragon eggs for the stupid ones?" He thumped the ground near her with his long, heavy tail.

"You do not like them, either?"

He snorted, ruffling the edge of her shawl. "Intolerable flitterbobs, just like those little fairy fluttertufts. But you seem to have a bit of sense to you. What are you doing here?"

"The Miss Delveses led me here, but they seem to have abandoned me. I do not think I was suitably frightened of the woods for their tastes."

Pembroke growled. That was a truly frightening sound. Elizabeth huddled under the shawl.

"Rise. You just may be tolerable—for a few moments."

Though it did not really sound like it, that was actually a great compliment from a basilisk.

Slowly, carefully, she pushed up to her knees, then stood, keeping her eyes down all the while. "I am honored that you should think so."

"I am Marchog Pembroke. You may address me." He lifted his head above hers and puffed to make his body larger.

He really did not need to do that. Everything about him was already quite impressive. She curtsied, touching her knee to the damp ground. "You honor me with your acquaintance."

"Indeed, I do. You intrigue me." He circled her once again, as though trying to make out what sort of creature she was. "The stupid ones know I am here. We have been introduced, yet they still shriek and shake when they see me. You do not, and yet you are smaller than they. Why?" He poked her with a taloned foot.

Gracious, those claws were remarkably long—he might be able to dig through some of the softer rock found in the hillsides with those. But he was very gentle with them; they tickled just a bit.

"I suppose you already know, Marchog." She giggled a little. "After all, you call them the stupid ones."

His yellow eyes widened and stared at her, huffing a sort of laughing sound. "You have no fear—of them, or of me."

"Pray do not be offended. You are a regal and terrifying creature, to be sure, and none should underestimate your power, or, I should think, your intellect. But I knew to expect you in these woods, so I was not surprised to see you. And I know the Blue Order keeps you from harming me, as long I do not threaten you. Truly, you could hardly consider me any kind of threat."

"Hardly. I have never met a warm-blood like you." The corner of his mouth lifted a little like a smile.

"I have read of the great basilisk, but I do not know if everything I have read is true. Would you condescend to tell me more about yourself? I am certain you have seen many wonderful things."

"You are a very peculiar little thing, to be sure, but interesting. Far more interesting than any I have spoken to in a long time. You are a guest of the house, though, and if you do not return before the sun sets, my woods are likely to be overrun with more trespass-ers. I will take you to where you can see the house again—and I shall talk to you as we walk." He nudged her to follow as he slunk past.

It was easy to see how some could view Pembroke as frightening, but he really was a very gracious crea-ture, telling her so many fascinating stories as they walked back. Moreover, he introduced her to Master Delves, older brother to the Miss Delveses, who had gotten as far as the edge of the garden in his quest to look for her.

The following day, Elizabeth spent no less than an hour wandering the corridors of the manor, trying to find the parlor where the Delves sisters were supposed to meet her. By the time she was able to find a maid who took her there, the sisters declared they had to leave to attend a social call and fled the room. Did they really have a call to pay, or were they embarrassed to face her after what they had done? In either case, how was she to teach them about fairy dragons if they avoided her?

At least their absence had given her an excellent ex-cuse to observe the tatzelwurms in the barn. They were different to the ones that lived in the Longbourn barns. These were gingery-colored and far friendlier. Three young ones—what did one call young tatzelwurms? "Wyrmlings" sounded odd to the ear, but it was a sweet sounding name for very adorable little creatures. Their talons were scratchy—they had not learned to curb them yet. But the delight of having them climbing over her, purring and rubbing their heads under her chin, was worth the scratches she now sported on her arms and legs. Their brood mother seemed to have the same sort of disposition, and a bit more sense than her brood. She sat beside them, encouraging their antics, and telling Elizabeth tales of life on Pembroke that painted Sir Rowley as a kindhearted Keeper.

Considering his daughters' dispositions, it was a comfort to know that there would be someone who would be concerned over the little fairy dragons' needs.

Two mornings later, Elizabeth made it to the morning room, thanks to a careful set of directions given to her by the housekeeper herself. It was a large, cheerful chamber with walls the color of sunshine. Mahogany furniture with long, lean lines graced the room in the form of sideboards laden with breakfast food, chairs around the table, and a pair of small tables near the window. A soft breeze gusted playfully through pale yellow curtains, leaving them dancing in its wake. If a room could feel happy, then this one did—it all but smiled at them.

She sat at the far end of the large, oblong table, well away from Papa and Sir Rowley. She opened her commonplace book and started to write about her latest tatzelwurm observations, but it was nearly impossible not to hear their conversation.

"I hear you got some very welcome news from the Order recently." Sir Rowley refilled Papa's coffee cup. "I cannot say I am surprised. I expect you are their leading candidate."

Papa dipped his head slightly with a quick, not quite warning, glance at Elizabeth. "I am honored that they would consider me."

"But not surprised." He clapped Papa's shoulder. "None of us are. Who would be? There could hardly be another man in the running who could match your expertise."

"There are not many in the running at all." Papa took a long sip from his cup and set it aside.

Sir Rowley laughed heartily. "True enough, but why dwell upon that? You know that is only because the position requires—"

"A peculiar disposition, a penchant for minute details, and a preference for dusty libraries to interacting with society."

Whatever they were talking about seemed to fit Papa very well, indeed. Elizabeth sat up very straight, but did not look toward them.

"There is more to you than that, Bennet, but I grant, it does describe you rather well. Congratulations. When will the official decision be made? I want to make certain I am there to see it. Can you imagine what our old university chums would say to it?"

"Considering that none of them heard dragons, they would probably think I had finally gone quite daft—devoting myself to studying and preserving the lore of fantastical creatures that have never existed." Papa grunted and returned to his coffee. "The decision will probably not be made for several months. And even when it is, I do not anticipate a great brouhaha being made over it. There is little point in calling a Conclave for such a mundane matter, for which I will be quite content."

"Not wanting to jump into the society spotlight? Just like you. Never met another man so averse to society. My wife would never tolerate such from me."

How many times had Mama complained of just

that?

"I do not expect there will be much socializing, whatever comes of this. I have never exactly been the one who is favored at parties, always smelling like dust and old books, after all. I see no need to worry that my wife will become suspicious of my many absences."

Sir Rowley wandered to the sideboard and piled a plate with cold ham and some sort of red fruit preserves. "You will never change, will you?"

"No, not any more than your estate dragon will."

Pembroke was definitely not one to embrace change well. But he was not nearly so—

"Speaking of which, Miss Elizabeth—"

Elizabeth jumped.

"Do you believe my daughters are prepared for the hatching?"

"We are, Papa!" Miss Eva burst into the morning room, her sisters just behind. "Miss Elizabeth has spoken of nearly nothing but fairy dragons all the time we have been together."

In an odd sort of way, that statement was true, although it implied something that was altogether false. Was she telling the truth or not? It did not seem so, but it was a very interesting way to lie.

"Indeed, she is a little font of knowledge. I am quite certain I do not know how she can possibly know so very much. Surely more than I will ever know myself." Miss Delves sat beside her father, sneaking a glance Elizabeth's way that would turn a basilisk to stone.

Apparently, Miss Delves had learned more from Pembroke than she had realized.

"But do you understand what will be required of you?" Papa's tone suggested that perhaps he was not fooled by the girl's insistence. At least, he was not directing it toward Elizabeth.

"I am quite sure we do." Miss Elaine sat near her father, a plate of toast in her hand.

Elizabeth pressed her lips and contained her sigh, but she arranged her face into a pleasing expression.

"Is it true, Papa, that we are to be going to London soon?" Miss Delves was obviously trying to sound very unconcerned regarding the matter.

"After the dragons are old enough to safely travel that distance. Bennet says it usually takes a month or so. You need have no fear about missing the season. The dragons will not interfere with your come-out."

"But a whole month?" Miss Delves pouted just a bit. "Mama said we should get to London early to have time to visit the dressmakers and milliners. I do not yet have the clothes—"

Papa clutched his forehead and covered his eyes. "I assure you, the young dragons are so demanding that you will hardly notice the time. You will be kept very busy, especially during the first several days after hatching."

Miss Delves did not look relieved, or even pleased.

"I am sure once your little friends arrive, you will hardly want to go anywhere." Sir Rowley patted his daughter's hand.

Running steps approached from the hallway, "Father!" Master Delves burst into the morning room. He was a shorter, rounder version of his father, with a remarkably similar disposition. He had been very kind and gracious to Elizabeth when he had escorted her back to the house. "It is time! It is time!"

Everyone but Papa jumped.

"There is no need to run. It will not happen so suddenly." He rose and set his napkin aside.

Sir Rowley led his chittering daughters out, his son following. Had they any idea they sounded much like a harem of fairy dragons following their lead male? They probably would not approve of the comparison.

"Come along, Elizabeth. But pray, try to stay out of the way and do not interfere. I have a suspicion the girls may be rather excitable. It seems their brother wishes to observe as well, so the room will be quite crowded. The chicks may not find the environment to their liking, and if they wish to leave, they must be allowed to do so." His tone suggested he rather expected it.

"But they will be so small! Do they not need help?"

"Those that are strong enough will survive, and those that are not—well, they would not help their species by doing so."

"Yes, Papa." She swallowed hard.

There was no point in arguing. This was the way of things. Still though, she did not have to like it. She followed him down the long, winding corridor to Sir Rowley's study.

Chapter 6

The nesting box rested on a low table near the fireplace in the middle of a happy sunbeam that poured through the nearest window. A very agreeable situation for the eggs as fairy dragons loved to play in the sunshine. The young Delveses surrounded the nesting box, with their father standing slightly behind his son. The girls whispered among themselves. Elizabeth chose not to listen as it would be rude, but they sounded very silly indeed.

Papa stationed himself slightly apart from them, nearer to the desk. He waved Elizabeth toward the corner, near the hob. "Elizabeth, slice the blood pudding into that dish and add some hot water from the hob."

She hurried there. How pleasant it was that she did not have to duck and dodge around piles of books and other obstacles to get there. Perhaps Papa might give her the arranging of his study when they returned.

Maybe she would be able to make it more like this one. Perhaps he would be less cross if he had less difficulty finding what he was looking for.

It was not likely, but one could hope.

Miss Eva leaned close to Miss Elaine and muttered, "I thought they ate nectar."

"Many develop that preference, but blood pudding in broth is an excellent first meal for all of them." Papa sounded so calm and pleasant, but that tone really meant that he was becoming irritated.

Miss Eva stared at him with wide eyes. Though his joints might be failing him, his hearing was even keener than the typical Dragon Keeper's.

It probably was not polite to stare at Miss Eva. Best attend to what he had asked her to do. If the food was not ready when they needed it, Papa would be most unhappy. He might even put her out of the room for it. That was not a risk worth taking. Taking the little silver knife Papa had laid out for her, she shaved the pudding into the hot water.

The thin slivers of pudding turned the water dark, a little like soup. It did not smell very appealing, though. Generally, she preferred not to eat blood pudding. It was difficult to imagine the little dragons liking it. But Papa was certain. Perhaps the little dragons would like it better if there were something sweet added to it. She would have to ask him later.

"Oh, the eggs are quivering!" Miss Eva squealed and pointed.

The three faintly blue speckled eggs rocked, each at their own pace near the center of the box. Should someone separate them a bit so they did not knock into one another?

"Ladle some broth and sausage into these saucers,

Lizzy." Papa placed an oblong wooden tray near her which bore three deep saucers designed for chocolate. How clever! With the rail in the center of the saucer, the broth could be contained, and the little dragons would have a place to perch while eating.

Elizabeth filled the saucers and brought the tray within reach of the nesting box.

"It is important you do not free them from their shells too soon. The exercise is necessary for them—it could kill them if you deprive them of it. Once their wings are free, then you may assist them." Papa folded his arms over his chest and spoke with a voice of authority.

The young Delveses nodded somberly. Finally, it appeared they were listening to something.

"And take these," Papa handed out frayed grey flannel rags. "They will need to be dried once they have hatched, lest they take a chill. They are so small. Cold will be a danger to them."

Elizabeth glanced over her shoulder. The fireplace held enough of a fire to keep the room warm for them. The windows were shut against a draught. That would help to keep the babies warm.

"Look! Look!" Miss Delves pointed at the center-most egg.

It fell over, and a tiny pointed beak appeared.

"That is the way, little one," Elizabeth murmured. The egg rolled toward her a bit, and a needle-sharp dark-streaked beak pressed further out.

A wet, matted head appeared. The chick was some shade of blue, darker now—because of the egg slime— than it would be when it fully dried, soft and fluffy and adorable.

It cried a tiny shriek, and the egg tore open. The

little dragon tumbled out.

"Oh! Oh! It is slimy and awful!" Miss Eva jumped to her feet. "I cannot abide slimy things!" She dashed from the room.

Elizabeth half-rose, but Papa stayed her with a shake of his head. "Leave her go. She is clearly not ready for this."

Miss Elaine reached out to the tiny chick and tried to pick her up—the head shape was distinctly female—but the chick screeched and pecked her hand.

"Ouch! You did not say these creatures were dangerous!" She yanked her hand back and put her stuck finger in her mouth.

"They are dragons!" Elizabeth huffed, eyes bulging. No, that was probably not an appropriate thing to say, but really, what did the daft girl expect? Kittens? Even they had sharp little teeth and claws.

"They are supposed to be tame and gentle. I want nothing of this!" Miss Elaine tossed her head and her skirts as she stormed from the room.

Elizabeth did not bother watching her leave.

Sir Rowley's eyebrows scrunched down over his eyes as his lips bunched into a frown.

"Companion dragons are not for the faint of heart. Some are surprised by the experience, even though they may have been told what to expect." Papa raised an eyebrow in her direction.

Elizabeth shrugged. She had tried, very diligently to instruct the girls. Was it her fault they would not attend?

"What should I do?" Miss Delves whispered, hands trembling.

"Extend the flannel to the chick and allow her to accept your help." Papa peered over her shoulder.

Squawks came from the other two eggs and tiny beaks pierced the shells. Moments later two more chicks, a pale pink female and a burgundy male—gracious! Males were uncommon!—tumbled out from their shells. The pink one staggered toward Miss Delves' proffered flannel and fell into it. She gently cleaned the chick.

Papa nudged Master Delves. "Go ahead and assist the little male."

Wonder in his eyes, Master Delves ministered to the burgundy chick who trilled at the attention. No doubt there was a Friendship forming there. Something about the way he handled the baby—he would be an excellent Dragon Mate.

The blue one hopped away from the others, toward the fireplace. Poor little thing was cold.

"Papa?"

He handed her a flannel, a little frown creasing the edges of his mouth. But it was not the expression he used when he was exasperated with her, so she took the cloth and offered it to the chick. She grabbed it in her tiny beak and tried to dab her wings with it, but to little effect.

"May I help you?" Elizabeth held her hand out only for the chick to peck it sharply. It stung a bit but no more than a pin prick. What a ninny Miss Elaine was for reacting to it so!

The chick pecked twice more, then puffed herself out just a bit, a very grumpy look on her face, and pushed the flannel into Elizabeth's hand. She scrubbed the slime off the fairy dragon's face.

"That one is in no want of a Friend. Sometimes that is their disposition. Still, it is not a bad thing that it will have imprinted on people at hatching," Papa said softly, looking toward Sir Rowley.

"Once they are clean and dry, offer them the saucers of the blood pudding and broth." Papa set saucers near all three of them.

The blue chick pouffed up into a lovely iridescent turquoise ball of fluff—round and soft as a little dandelion. Her little black eyes glittered like jet beads, bright and intelligent. She jumped on to Elizabeth's hand, clinging with very sharp toes, and shrieking at what must have been the top of her tiny lungs.

"Dragon's blood, child! Offer her food!" Papa grabbed the saucer and held it near Elizabeth's hand.

The chick tipped her beak into the broth and screamed violently, batting at the saucer. It toppled from Papa's hand, into the nesting box.

"What an awful creature!" Miss Delves edged away, her little pink fluff ball perched daintily on the edge of the saucer, sipping broth without spilling a drop, as elegant a young lady as her new Friend.

Papa pinched the bridge of his nose.

The blue one shrieked again.

"Poor thing sounds hungry." Master Delves winced as the burgundy pouf tightened tiny piercing toes around his finger. "Why does she refuse the broth?"

"Pray, Sir Rowley," Elizabeth turned away from Papa, "have you any honey, or preserves, or even treacle in reach?"

He trundled to his desk. "Just in luck, the housekeeper failed to take this back to the kitchen after I last took tea."

He handed Elizabeth a small china honey-pot. She held it out, and the blue chick nearly fell face first into the pot.

"There, there now, no need to be so greedy. No one

is going to take this away from you. Slow down, or you will choke." Elizabeth pulled the chick back from the pot until she swallowed, despite the needle toes scratching at her hands. "See, you may have as much as you like, only slowly, lest you make yourself sick." She brought the pot toward the chick again.

Halfway through the honey, the chick's gluttony subsided, and she reverted to dainty swallows, more typical of her kind. When only a quarter remained in the pot, she pulled away and began to clean herself with her long forked tongue.

Elizabeth giggled only to receive another sharp peck on the hand.

"I do not like being laughed at." The blue chick scolded, her voice so high and thin that Elizabeth was not certain she had heard.

"I do not like being pecked at. I suppose we must all endure things we do not like very much."

Master Delves gasped and pressed his fist to his mouth.

"You are awfully bold for a warm-blood." The chick scratched beside her beak with her foot and licked bits of honey from her toes.

Elizabeth held her up to look eye to eye with her. "And you are awfully bold for such a very young and adorable dragon."

The little blue puff snorted and sneezed. "That is hardly likely to change."

"No, I expect not." They locked gazes. There was something very sympathetic in the young dragon's eyes. She was not like the rest of her kind, a little like Elizabeth was unlike her sisters.

Papa grunted at her and looked toward the window. When had he opened it?

Elizabeth swallowed hard and sighed. He was right. It was the proper thing to do, even if it was unlikely that a chick would survive on its own after hatching. But this one was different. She just might. "I suppose you will be wanting to leave now?"

Turquoise fluff fluttered in the breeze as her tiny head turned to and fro. "No."

"Excuse me?" Papa leaned over Elizabeth's shoulder.

"No. She will do for me."

What had she just said? Elizabeth's knees wobbled.

"But she is too young, not even part of the Order." Papa tried his authoritative tone, but the little dragon turned her head aside.

"What Order? I am tired. Get out of my way." She hopped up Elizabeth's arm and tucked herself under Elizabeth's shawl, against her neck. Her soft feather scales prickled and tickled.

He dragged his hand down his face, muttering, "She is every bit as stubborn as you are."

The chick peeked out from beneath the shawl. "Then we will be very good Friends."

"What shall we call you?" Elizabeth cupped her hand over the tiny fairy dragon. "I do not imagine you will want a name of my offering."

"When does it begin getting warm again? I do not like this cold." She pressed a little harder against Elizabeth's warmth.

"Spring begins in March, but usually in April it is more reliably pleasant."

"Then I shall be April."

"Does that mean you shall also be reliably pleasant?"

"No. Does that bother you?"

"Should it?" Truthfully, no one at Longbourn was reliably pleasant.

April pulled the shawl over her head. A moment later, sweet little snores bubbled from underneath.

Sir Rowley clapped Papa's shoulder. "It seems you have a fairy dragon in the Keep now."

Papa shook his head and grumbled. "You have made this very difficult for me."

Elizabeth looked up at him, covering April with her palm again. "I asked her if she wanted to leave, but she did not. I did nothing to make her stay. She does not like the cold."

"Do not torment the girl, Bennet. You know it was not her fault. Dragons will do what dragons will do. Think of it this way: I now have two in the family—and one seems quite attached to my son! How am I going to explain that? Men do not befriend fairy dragons."

"His name is Port, for he is the color of port wine." Master Delves winked at her.

"Port is a male—does not that make a difference?" Elizabeth asked.

"It might, but I do not care. When one keeps a basilisk, one does not expect a great deal of draconic companionship, so I am very happy to have a Dragon Friend of any ilk." He stroked Port's fluffy head.

"You see, Bennet, if I can be content with such Friends in my family, then you can be as well." Sir Rowley strode toward the cabinet containing his liquor decanters.

"But your entire family can hear. You do not understand what a trial a family that does not hear can be. Truly, trying to prevent my wife from discovering dragons is an imposition you cannot begin to comprehend.

You know her—she could never have been accepted as a Deaf Speaker."

But if that was such a problem, why did he marry Mama in the first place? Would that not be rather short-sighted?

"I do not imagine that to be the biggest problem," April whispered in her ear.

"You should not say such things," Elizabeth murmured back.

"Why not?"

"It is considered rude. Besides, you have never even met Mama."

April snorted.

"Papa will insist—you must learn manners if you are to stay with us. There is no choice." Elizabeth peeked at Papa who rolled his eyes.

"You will feed me properly?"

"Of course, I will."

"Then I supposed I can be well-mannered—when I have to," April murmured just loud enough to be heard by all.

Sir Rowley laughed heartily. "You see, there, she has promised to act properly."

"Pray sir, do not laugh at her. She does not like it." Elizabeth tucked her shawl firmly around April lest she try to peck at their host.

She poked her head out through Elizabeth's fingers, growling. "No, I do not."

It was not right that a growl should be so precious, but it was.

Papa had not warned her about the "days of great hunger" as she called them in her commonplace book, in the very few moments she had to write in it. But why would he have? She was not to have befriended a fairy dragon. Moreover, the intense inconvenience of it all might have discouraged the Miss Delveses from befriending the little dragons. For three days, she and Miss Delves—now Emily as the entire affair had put them on a first-name basis—shared a chamber with the two chicks, Rose and April, where it seemed they did nothing but feed, preen, and sleep with the little dragons.

In the odd moments of stillness, they talked about dragons. Emily suddenly wanted to know everything Elizabeth was supposed to have already taught her. Apparently what the Miss Delveses had to learn for acceptance testing into the Blue Order contained precious little about fairy dragons. For Rose's sake, Elizabeth obliged, though she was still wary about trying to tell the older girl anything. But this time, Emily listened and even made notes. Apparently having a tiny dragon Friend was already improving Emily's disposition. Perhaps April might have some of the same effect on Mama.

Papa had already decided they would tell her that April was a gift from Sir Rowley, a rare sort of hummingbird. Elizabeth could hardly refuse such a gift without offending the baronet. That should obtain Mama's approbation readily enough. The very mention of rank made Mama ready to please. However, she was not their only problem.

All minor dragons who were to be members of the Keep had to be presented to Longbourn. Apparently, he had a long history of jealousy and ill-temper and had not been in the habit of accepting Keep mates in a very long time. Was that the real reason there was no household Dragon Friend at Longbourn? Papa would have to introduce Elizabeth to Longbourn sooner than he had intended to and ask him to accept April into the Keep. If Longbourn said "no"—well, they would have a problem on their hands.

Perhaps she might go to live with Uncle Gardiner and his new wife—they were to be married soon. She would no doubt find April adorable, and Rustle could hardly object. He was a crusty old creature, but not cruel enough to put out a little baby to fend for itself. Since the Gardiners would probably have a baby soon—that is what newly married couples did, after all—perhaps Elizabeth could offer to help with the baby. Perhaps they would not even need a nursery maid if she did. Hopefully, she would not have to resort to leaving home, but regardless of Longbourn, she would not turn April out. That was all there was to the conversation, even though Papa did not yet know it.

On the fifth day after hatching, Papa planned to go home, after breakfast. That would put them back at Longbourn near dinner, and Mama would have less time for questions—or complaints. Those could wait until morning, after Papa had time to judge her mood and decide on the best approach to convincing her to accept April.

Elizabeth awoke at sunrise, April nestled under her chin. Her feather-scales were fluffy and a little itchy, but she snored very sweetly, and her presence was somehow very comforting, so Elizabeth bore it without complaint. A high-necked nightgown would likely remedy the problem quickly. She would alter her existing ones easily enough when she got home. Mama would probably be glad to see her sewing without being nagged to do so.

"We need to take our leave of Pembroke." Elizabeth slipped out of bed, placing April on the pillow where she had been lying.

"At sunrise? Wait at least until it is warmer." April slipped under the blanket.

"Come along, now. I do not know how long this will take, and Papa will be very angry if our errand causes our departure to be late."

"Then go without me. I want to sleep."

"You were hatched here. You should be introduced to Pembroke. It is only proper, and one never knows when it will be handy to have a particular acquaintance." Elizabeth pulled her dress over her head.

"He will not recognize me, anyway. I am too small." The blanket muffled April's tiny voice.

"In size, perhaps, but not in courage. I think he will like you very well."

"And if he does not, he will eat me."

"No, he will not. I will protect you." Elizabeth released her hair from its braid and brushed it.

"He might eat you, too. You said he was a large dragon."

"Landed dragons do not randomly eat girls—or anyone else. It is against the laws of the Blue Order. Besides, we have already shared a very pleasant conversation. He has intriguing stories to tell."

April peeked out above the covers. "I am hungry."

Elizabeth opened a small jar on the bedside table. "I have a pot of jam for you, and a bit of dried fruit. I saw a few flowers in the garden hot house. Perhaps you might sample some of their nectar on the way."

April hopped to the pot of jam. "Flowers do sound awfully nice. I suppose I shall go with you."

"Of course, you shall. Now eat as I finish with my hair."

Half an hour later, Elizabeth wrapped her shawl over her shoulders and April snuggled underneath, near the side of her neck. A cape, with a hood designed to accommodate the fairy dragon, would be so much more convenient. Another project to sew when she returned home.

After a stop at the hothouse, where April gorged herself among the blossoms, Elizabeth picked her way along the stream to Pembroke's domain. So early in the morning, the path was much brighter and cheerier than late in the afternoon. Maybe if the Miss Delveses met him like this, they would like him better.

"Marchog Pembroke!" Closing her eyes, she could just make out the slithering sound he made as he approached. He must be dragging his tail to make that sound. His footfalls were all but silent. She knelt and covered herself with her shawl.

"You have returned? Why?" He sounded more amused than annoyed.

"Three fairy dragons hatched on your Keep. Two of them, called Rose and Port, shall be presented to you soon to be accepted into your Keep."

Pembroke snorted as though he had a fairy dragon up his nose. "I have no use for fluttertufts on my Keep."

April poked her head out and shrieked at him, hopping from one foot to the other on Elizabeth's shoulder. It was probably a good thing she had not yet learned to fly. "How dare you call me a flitterspot!"

Pembroke strode closer, forked tongue flicking, tasting the air. "Fluttertuft."

"Fluffertip?" April stopped hopping and turned her

head almost sideways.

"Fluttertuft."

"Floofersport?"

His long tongue reached for April. She pecked at it, landing one sharp blow with her beak.

Elizabeth covered her with her palm. "Pray forgive her, Pembroke; she is just a baby!"

Pembroke laughed that same odd huffing sound he had made the last time she had seen him. "A baby what? She seems more cockatrix than fairy dragon."

April forced her head between Elizabeth's fingers. "Thank you. I would thank you to remember that."

Pembroke tossed his head back and laughed again, this time a deeper, growly sort of reverberation that could have sounded menacing without the draconic fanged smile to go with it. "I will not forget. Is the blue one to stay as well?"

"No." April snorted.

"Her name is April, and she has decided she will be going home with me. If, of course, you will permit her to leave."

"Permit me?" April pecked at her hand. "I do not need—"

Elizabeth covered her with both hands. "By your leave, Marchog."

"Granted. If the other two are of her ilk, they may well be worth having about. I may just choose to receive them."

"I—we—are honored." Elizabeth curtsied.

Pembroke stepped closer to her, almost touching her skirts. "I will walk with you toward the house. Send my Keeper to me when you arrive. I would discuss the matter with him."

"I am sure he will be very pleased to receive your

summons."

"No, he will not. But little matter. I am not here to serve his convenience."

"Were you born to this estate?" Elizabeth asked.

"That is an interesting story. I will tell you as we walk."

What stories the basilisk had to tell! Pray the coach ride would be steady enough that she might write them down as they traveled. She could not risk forgetting anything. Considering how grouchy basilisks were said to be, he was quite personable, even gracious. Certainly, he had little patience for what he considered silly or stupid, but that was only to be expected. When one was three hundred years old, one had little patience for anything annoying.

Once at the manor, she went straight to the morning room. Sir Rowley and Papa sipped coffee and spoke in soft tones, the kind she was not supposed to overhear, but her preternatural hearing allowed her to detect nonetheless. Best accomplish her errand quickly before she heard something she should not.

"Pray excuse me, sir." She curtsied as she entered the room. "Marchog Pembroke has requested your presence, sir."

Sir Rowley jumped and nearly dropped his cup. Papa's eyes grew very wide.

"Pembroke has seen you, spoken with you?" Something in Sir Rowley's voice suggested that it would be a very bad idea to say yes.

"I was given the message by a … forest wyrm, sir. It seemed rather agitated and hopeful to discharge the assignment to anyone else." That should be entirely believable, for wyrms were flighty that way. It was not right to lie, of course, but the truth seemed like a worse idea just at the moment. April nodded against the side of her neck, hidden by the shawl, as though she had the same thought.

"I see." Sir Rowley stroked his chin, still looking a bit skeptical. "I suppose he has gotten wind of the fairy dragons hatching. There seems to be no keeping secrets from an estate dragon."

Papa leaned his elbows on the table. "You did not tell him of the whole affair before we arrived?"

"I find with Pembroke it is more expedient to tell him of such things after the fact. It saves a great deal of snorting and stomping and threatening and negotiating."

Elizabeth bit her tongue. What would they care that she thought it was a dreadful way to treat one who was supposed to be a friend and ally?

"You will excuse me, Bennet?" Sir Rowley rose.

"Of course. It is time for us to be leaving in any case. Lizzy, have yourself a bite of breakfast, and be quick about it. I am sure the carriage is nearly ready for us." Papa followed Sir Rowley out.

Did he suspect the truth about Pembroke? He certainly could not address that here. She would probably find out in the carriage. She climbed onto a chair and ate. April popped out from under the shawl and jumped onto the table, hopping to and fro looking for something sweet. How could she possibly be hungry again after all those preserves and the flower nectar?

Half an hour later, the driver handed her into the carriage and Papa climbed in behind her. April complained only slightly, though she refused to ride within the little padded box Sir Rowley had provided for her.

Papa sighed, but apparently decided that the argument with April was not worth the possible reward. One had to have a very good reason to argue with a dragon.

"I do not know how we are going to deal with your mother. I fear she will be put out that you have such a pretty gift, while Jane has nothing of the sort. She might even insist that Jane begin to travel with me as it is unfair that you are the only one to come."

"But Jane does not like to copy for you, and her hand is not so accurate as mine."

"Nor does she hear dragons, but I can hardly explain that to either of them." He clapped his forehead and shook his head. "I am not certain your handwriting will be enough to overcome the possibility for connections and trinkets."

"You fret far too much. I will manage her." April bobbed her head, entirely confident in herself. "She does not sound like a woman difficult to persuade. Neither of them do."

"You have only just hatched—what would you know of persuasion?" Papa folded his arms over his chest and glowered.

"Did you not notice how the maid brought the pot of strawberry preserves and placed it right next to you when I asked?" April cocked her head—was that an expression of pride?

"She was not a hearer?"

"Hardly."

"Acquiring a pot of sweets is not the same as managing a household." Papa leaned his head back into the lumpy squabs.

"I am quite sure I can manage." April turned her tail to him and ducked under Elizabeth's shawl.

The coach lurched into motion. Papa did not say anything for the first quarter hour. That, in and of itself, was nothing unusual. Elizabeth took out her commonplace book and pencil and began to write, though the lurching carriage made her handwriting awful.

"I will have to write to the Order directly—or rather, have you take down the letter for me. You cannot really be a Dragon Friend without belonging to the Order as the Misses Delves do. This is all out of order, you realize." He spoke to the ceiling.

"I am sorry, Papa."

"There are standards, you know, standards which you must conform to, despite your age. Technically, you are too young to be a part, but April's impulsive choice now requires the Order to look beyond that. However, you must still satisfy all their other demands."

"What must I do?" She shut her book and laced her fingers tightly.

"Primarily, you must study to pass the tests they will require of you. You must learn all of the history of the Order and the contents of the Pendragon Treaty and the Accords. You must demonstrate that you understand how to behave among those who do not hear and that you are in no way a danger to the secrecy of dragonkind. I had hoped to shield you from this until you were older, and more able to manage the task, as Delves' daughters were. But now the issue has been forced."

She stared at her fingernails. How was she to know this Friendship would have been so difficult for Papa?

But if the Miss Delveses were accepted into the Order, why should she not be? She knew far more than they did and was willing to study and learn whatever was required. Perhaps, because of their rank, they were permitted a less rigorous process? Even if that were the case, she would do whatever it took to ensure the Order admitted her, too.

"I know that she chose you, Lizzy, and there is little to be done for it." He glared at April. "What is done is done now. But you must understand—you must both understand—that dragons are not safe creatures. They are not by their nature friendly, and some are not even trustworthy. One must tread very carefully amongst them if one is to live in their world."

"I understand, truly I do." But Longbourn and Pembroke had been so amenable; surely he was exaggerating.

"I hardly think that is possible. But, I do believe you want to understand."

"I will study very hard. I will make you proud of me."

April peeked out from the shawl. "What will happen if she does not?"

Could she not see that was not a question to be asked right now?

"We shall not think of that right now. I have confidence in you, and we shall do everything in our power to make sure that does not happen." He leaned back and closed his eyes.

April drew a breath to speak, but Elizabeth covered her with her palm. "He wants to rest now. Do not disturb him."

"But—"

"You must trust me. There are times when it is best to hold one's tongue. Now is one of those."

April huffed and puffed her feather-scales, but did

not speak.

Papa was worried, but he need not be. She had already met major dragons without incident. Rumblkins liked her and sought her out readily enough, and now April was her Friend. There was nothing to fear. It would be well. She would prove that to him.

Chapter 7

As Papa had predicted, Mama was none too happy to have Elizabeth bring home a pet. In the first place, she had no great love for birds—a dog would be far more appropriate to life in the country—and in the second, as the eldest, Jane should have been offered the privilege first. Jane, as anyone who knew her would expect, was genuinely happy for Elizabeth's good fortune, and was not in the least bit jealous. Her younger sisters seemed indifferent, especially once they saw how much effort went into April's care.

Happily, though, Mama proved quite susceptible to April's persuasion. In short order, she had conceded that April's song was indeed very pleasant and seemed to calm Lydia's temper when nothing else would. On the strength of that recommendation alone, Mama decided April could stay—for the time being at least.

In the ensuing weeks, April settled into the rhythms

of the household until the non-hearing members of the family barely noticed her presence. Would that Papa could be equally content with the results. But no, it seemed he had become even grumpier than ever.

At least his moods provided a good excuse to remain above stairs, ensconced in her room with April, helping her to learn to fly, recording observations in her commonplace book, and trying her hand at some needlework she would normally have avoided.

November 1802

A cold breeze whistled past and rattled the windows of her room as Elizabeth fastened the deep green wool cloak over her shoulders for the first time. Grey clouds passed over the sun, obscuring the light, but just for a moment. The light resumed, and she turned this way and that in front of the long mirror, admiring the way the heavy fabric draped along her back and swung to and fro as she walked. Yes, it would do very well.

She folded the hood across her shoulders and laid the wide collar over it, smoothing it carefully. "Are you ready to render your opinion?"

April twittered from her perch atop the mirror. "How is this so very different from your old one?" She flitted to Elizabeth's shoulder.

Her flight was still a bit wobbly and clearly effortful, but a great improvement from even just a se'nnight ago. Soon she would be able to soar about without even thinking about it. Was this how a mother felt when her infant first learned to walk?

"Well, they are both handed down from Jane, so I understand how they would look very similar. But see how I have altered the hood and collar just for your comfort." Elizabeth pointed to the deep pleats just behind her neck.

April rooted around in the folds of the hood and under the collar, tickling Elizabeth as she went. "You have added more fabric so the gathers are very generous, and the hood is so very soft." She snuggled into it.

"That is because I made a new hood from the scraps of green velvet from Mama's new pelisse. I used the hood fabric to make another panel to add fullness to the cloak."

The entire affair was of her own design, of which Mama would certainly not have approved had she known Elizabeth's intent. But thanks to April's intervention, she never asked. Instead, Mama was surprised and pleased that Elizabeth had finally shown a proper interest in sewing.

"I like it. It is very cozy. I can go out with you, and none shall notice I am here—particularly your nosy mother." April wormed her way under the collar, pulling it to cover herself with her sharp beak.

"Do not talk about Mama that way." Elizabeth turned her side to the mirror. April was nearly invisible in her hiding place, just as she intended.

April poked her head out and chirruped in Elizabeth's ear. "But it is true! She inserts herself into the matters of dragons where she has absolutely no business. That is nosy. What is more, she is opinionated. Who is she to declare you did not need a new cloak to accommodate me?"

Elizabeth turned her face away from the mirror to hide the way she rolled her eyes. April did not appreciate that expression. "That matter was adequately resolved, was it not?"

"I did not like convincing her that your elder sister

required a new cloak when, in fact, it was you who did."

"It was better that way. How else might I have acquired a garment of my own design?"

"I still do not like it." April harrumphed with her entire body. The expression was far too adorable to take seriously—a point which irritated April to no end.

Elizabeth picked up her bonnet from the top of the press. "We should go for a walk and try it out."

"But it is cold." April shivered within the hood.

Heavens, she could be as dramatic as Lydia!

"Of course, one does not wear a cloak when it is warm! The purpose of a cloak is to keep one warm—in this case, both of us. It is important to ensure it accomplishes that."

"I do not like the cold."

"It is a fact of life. When you are older, you can hibernate through the cold season if you wish." Elizabeth tied her bonnet ribbons.

"And miss everything that is going on? Thank you, no." April pulled a fold over her head and snorted.

Elizabeth giggled and headed for the stairs. April was like Lydia that way, too, ever afraid that she might miss something interesting or important. Neither of them liked to be kept to their chambers or even above stairs, and sleep was often an anathema!

While Papa found that trait quite trying, it was the way that April always spoke her mind that bothered him the most and left him muttering things like "rude" and "disrespectful" under his breath.

But why?

Was it not refreshing to have someone in one's life who always spoke the truth? Elizabeth might not always like what April had to say, but she never worried that April would suddenly change her story or deny she had ever said something. If anything, it made the little fairy dragon seem quite safe and reliable—at least, it did to her.

Papa, though, disliked that—*intensity,* he called it—and said it made April insolent and difficult to manage. Perhaps, he was right, a little, after a fashion. But it seemed more a matter of taste than anything else.

April suited her tastes very well, indeed.

Elizabeth pushed the kitchen door open and caught a crisp breeze full in the face. Oh, how it stung her nose and ears. She was not supposed to use that door—daughters of the house had no business in the kitchen, according to Mama. But Hill and Cook ignored her transgression, a touch of sympathy evident in the way they looked aside as she passed.

Elizabeth shrugged off a touch of guilt. It was not good to disobey Mama, but sometimes it really was necessary. How else could she avoid Mama and the requisite inspection of her needlework? Best make sure the cloak suited her needs before bothering Mama with it.

"Where are we going?" The cloak muffled April's voice.

"I do not know."

"You are lying." April pecked at her ear. "You are going to see Longbourn."

Ouch! Her beak seemed to have grown sharper over the last week. Elizabeth covered her ear with her hand. "What if I am? He does not object to my company."

"You father does not know you visit him."

"No, he does not." Elizabeth flipped the edge of her collar back over April's head.

"I heard your mother saying you were not 'out' in society, and that you could not talk to young males, or much of anyone at all."

"What has that to do with taking a walk?"

"I do not think you are 'out' to major dragons, either."

"There is no such thing as being 'out' to dragons."

April fluttered her wings and threw the collar off her head. "You father is likely to disagree. He might not call it by that name, but I am certain he feels so."

"Since when are you an advocate for his opinions? I thought it your sworn mission to constantly disagree with him. Besides, he is too late. I have already met Longbourn, and Pembroke, too—who was far more agreeable than his Keeper intimated he was. You met him for yourself."

"I do not think that is the material point—"

"It would be abominably rude to ignore the acquaintance now it has been made." Elizabeth crossed her arms and pulled the edges of the cloak closed over her chest.

April grumbled and burrowed deeper into the hood. Apparently that would be her newest way of ending a conversation. At least it was more agreeable than biting ears.

In truth, April had a point. Without a formal introduction to Longbourn, she should not be conversing with him. That was common courtesy—human courtesy, but courtesy nonetheless. On the other hand, Longbourn was the estate dragon, essentially family to the dragon-hearing Bennets. One did not need introductions to speak to family—unless they were very old and cranky persons of rank, which he was not—at least not exactly. Besides, it was hardly her fault that he introduced himself to her and continued finding excuses to catch her in regular conversation whilst she was out walking. One avoided denying a major dragon his desires whenever possible. Surely Papa would agree—he had been the one to teach her that principle, after all.

Bare skeletal branches reached over her head, forming a sort of arch above her. It looked rather like the frame for the barn Netherfield Park was building. Jane thought these woods spooky, even frightening, especially on days like today when the clouds made them even gloomier, and refused to walk through them with her. But that was probably just as well. Dragons never came out when Jane was along.

The trees thinned, like a crowd making way for a peer, as she approached the clearing where Longbourn usually met her. He almost always joined her when she came, but sometimes he did not, and she could not predict when that might be. So really, it was more of a chance meeting than anything else. How could Papa object to that?

She walked the perimeter of the clearing. A few tracks, which she recently learned were made by wyrms, crisscrossed the sandy soil. Were those the wyrms that Rumblkins had recently introduced her to? The long shaggy creatures, not much larger than Rumblkins, had lion-like faces and manes, with long fangs and bright eyes. They traveled in mated pairs, sometimes several pairs together—what did one call a large group of dragons? A flock? A herd? A school?—and were ever-so-silly. Their prattle sounded so much like Lydia when she was still in the nursery. Still though, they were jolly company, talking over one another to tell her about their adventures, especially when she carried treats with her or scratched their itchy ears.

Longbourn had been here recently, too. Those were his footprints and tail marks along the far side. Perhaps he would see her today.

She felt his steps through the soles of her shoes before she heard them. He was not thundering intentionally, at least not this time. He was just a big solid creature whose footfalls really were that heavy. But when he was stomping about in an irritated manner, one could not mistake what it was.

His scaly green head burst through the trees, and he peered at her as though trying to figure out what to do with her. Did he not recall that he knew her? Silly creature. She grabbed the bottom edges of her cloak and pulled it up, like wings, curtsied deeply and covered her head and face with the cloak. "Good day, Laird Longbourn."

He plodded closer, leaning down to sniff her. "Whatever are you doing?"

"Do you like my new cloak?" She dropped the edges, and it fell back into place as she twirled.

"What were you doing with it?"

"Those are my wings."

He snorted, ruffling the edges of her cloak. "You do not have wings. Girls do not have wings."

"I know that, silly. But dragons do, and they use them when they are greeting one another."

"Oh." He sat on his haunches and cocked his head, studying her. "Girls do not have wings. Why do you want wings?"

"Not just wings, but a hood, and a way to make myself big, you see. I want to be able to talk to dragons the right way."

He scratched behind his ear with his foot, a little like a very large dog scratching fleas. "I have never heard a warm-blood say such a thing."

April freed herself from the heavy cloak folds to

hover in front of Longbourn's face. "That is probably because one never has. I told her I thought it very peculiar."

Longbourn's eyes crossed a little as he tried to focus on April as she flew so close to his nose. "It is that."

"You do not approve?" Elizabeth swallowed hard, trying to keep the disappointment from her voice.

But she never had been very good at that. Mama often scolded her for it. It was unbecoming for a young woman to be so demonstrative.

"I did not say that." Longbourn blinked hard as April landed on his snout. Her scratchy toes tickled his thick hide. "I have simply never seen such a thing. I do not know what to make of it. Show me what you mean by talking to dragons right."

"Well, one principle of greeting, according to the book Papa gave me to study, is that the lesser dragon should appear as small as possible and, insofar as they are able, cover their fangs and talons and spikes and the like from the greater dragon. I thought by doing the same with my cloak, I might communicate the same deference of rank."

"Show me again." He wrinkled his lips in a thoughtful sort of pout.

She gathered up her cloak and curtsied again.

"I see the problem."

"Did I do it wrong?"

"A lesser dragon would not remain upright before a greater dragon. One must bring his head down very low."

Elizabeth peered up at him. "But I am already shorter than you are, and I will always be so."

"It is not a matter of absolute height, but of lowering oneself in the presence of the more powerful dragon. It is a demonstration that one will not attempt an attack, futile though it might be." The tip of his tail flicked as it did when he was thinking hard.

Her forehead furrowed, and she chewed her lip. The book had said nothing of the sort, but it made a great deal of sense. This was something to remember to add to her commonplace book. "So, I should do it more like this." She dropped her knees to the ground and pulled the cloak over her head.

"Yes, that is much better. That I recognize as a greeting from a lesser dragon, a clumsy, immature one, to be sure, but it makes the point rather clearly." He chuckled, a grumbly-growly sort of sound that was not an obvious sort of laugh. It had taken her some time to realize that was a sociable sound, not a dangerous one.

She dropped her head to her knees and wrapped her arms around her legs.

"What is wrong now?"

"I do not like to be laughed at."

He nudged her with his nose. "I do not mean to make you sad. I laugh because it is endearing."

"You mean silly." Considering Papa called Lydia, Kitty, and Mary—and Mama on occasion—silly, it was hardly a compliment.

"No, if I meant silly, I would have said it. It is charming that you are trying so hard to speak 'dragon.' It is not something warm-bloods are apt to try, much less succeed with."

"You think I succeeded?"

"Not quite yet, but I think you will, with some practice and instruction." He nudged her with his snout. "We will start now."

She clambered to her feet, holding her breath and biting her lip lest she say something to dissuade him.

"You will meet many more smaller dragons than you will larger ones, so you must be prepared to greet them, and show them you are the dominant dragon."

"Dominant? But I am just a girl."

"True enough, but to a little fluttertuft like her," Longbourn snorted and furrowed his nose, making April hop to keep her balance. "You are the dominant creature. Never doubt that—it will show in your greeting. Make it clear that you are the superior dragon immediately and garner their respect. Once you have it, then the precedent will be established, and you can expect a cordial acquaintance."

"I had no idea." Something else for her commonplace book, especially considering Papa's book of dragon greetings had so little to say about small minor dragons.

"We will begin with wyrms—"

"No!" April pecked his snout. "With fairy dragons. We are the smallest of the dragons, and the most plentiful. You should begin with us."

He crossed his eyes and bobbed his head. "Very well, with fairy dragons."

Once Longbourn became bored with teaching her how to greet—and establish dominance with—minor dragons, he dismissed her with a grouchy harrumph. When a large dragon harrumphed at one, it was difficult to ignore, but Longbourn's eyes crinkled up at the sides and there was something gentle and even pleased in his voice. Sometimes it seemed that his grouchy-dragon persona was more for show than it was a true reflection of him. It was annoying sometimes, but if people were concerned with keeping up appearances—

Mama certainly was—then how much more so might a major dragon be?

She hurried home, April tucked up in her hood against the chilly wind that had increased in the waning sunshine. Hopefully, she would not forget anything Longbourn had taught her along the way. Just in case, she murmured reminders under her breath.

"You missed a step," April twittered from deep in the green velvet hood.

"Which one?"

"I expect you will write this down when you get home. I will tell you then. Otherwise I will have to repeat myself, and I am in no mood for that."

"Just do not step on the wet ink this time." The little footprints she had left on the page were rather dear, but they did make some lines barely legible. April might not care about such things now, but if she ever learned to read, no doubt she would be offended if a page she had dictated proved difficult to make out.

Could fairy dragons learn to read? Every source she read considered them very stupid creatures. Had anyone ever tried to teach a fairy dragon to read?

"Give me a sheet of blotter paper to stand on then. Really, if you expect me to help you, you need to do a better job of making it easy for me to do so!"

She did have a point. A snippy, annoying little point, but a point nonetheless.

In the privacy—and warmth—of her room, Elizabeth placed her writing desk on the small table near the window and spread out her commonplace book. Did other dragon-hearing girls write of them in their commonplace books? Certainly, they must. What could be more important to write about? True, pretty quotations, receipts for lotions and balms, and advice from those learned in female conduct were important to record, but somehow that seemed to pale in comparison to far more important matters, such as the habits of tatzelwurms in the barns.

Perhaps one day, she might ask Emily what she wrote in her commonplace book now that she was Friends with Rose. But would such a question make it past Mama's inspection of her letters? She always read them before they were posted to make sure Elizabeth said nothing improper that might offend a friend so well-connected as Miss Delves. On the one hand, she could understand Mama's concern—especially in light of the need to keep up proper appearances—but on the other, it was a bit difficult, even offensive, to think that Mama believed her to have so little good sense as not to be able to write a letter to a particular friend without supervision. Perhaps a little help from April might ensure her question made it past Mama's inspection.

That was for later. Right now, she needed to make certain she accurately recorded what she had learnt today. She set out a piece of blotter paper and prepared her pen.

With April's help—or constant interference as it more often felt to be—she managed to record the last of Longbourn's instructions just before Mama called her and Jane down for supper. Mary, Kitty, and Lydia were, of course, too young to sup at the family table, but she insisted Jane and Elizabeth did—for it was never too early to instill proper etiquette in a young lady. She did not insist that they dress for dinner, at least not yet. Little girls did not have dinner dresses, after all. That would not happen until they were out in society.

Elizabeth capped the ink bottle, stood, and stretched. How long had she been at her writing desk? Long enough to make her shoulders ache and for nearly all of the sunlight to have disappeared behind the trees, making her squint at her paper. Perhaps it was a good time to stop, after all. She wrapped her shawl around her shoulders and made her way downstairs to the dining room just a few steps behind Jane.

How Mama loved her dining room! Two large mirrors, one above the fireplace and one on the opposite wall, multiplied the candlelight, making the room appear much brighter than the few candles would have ordinarily allowed. The table, dressed in bright white linen, was already laden with shiny serving dishes wafting inviting smells her way. Mama was known for setting an excellent table.

What did it mean to set an excellent table? Elizabeth had too little experience to know for certain. However, one thing was sure: the food served at the "big people's table" was far more palatable than the very bland stuff found at the nursery table, making dinner with Mama and Papa far and away more satisfying. Still though, dining in the nursery held one great appeal: one was free to engage in conversation during meals. In the dining room, one only spoke at Mama's bidding.

Today Mama was particularly talkative. She had seen Lady Lucas in town today and had a great deal to comment upon: her gown, her manners, how her eldest daughter, Charlotte, who was out in society, fared at the last assembly. Was it too early to hire a dance master to ensure that Jane—oh yes, and Lizzie, too, of course—were prepared to show themselves creditably when they began to dance in public.

Jane smiled pleasantly at the suggestion, and when

asked, offered a sweet and thoughtful remark on how well Charlotte must dance and how pleasant it must be to dance well. So very typical of Jane. How was it possible that anyone could be so sweet? Even April occasionally found Jane too sweet, which, considering April's love of honey and preserves, was saying something. But Jane's answer pleased Mama, and was very proper according to all the conduct writers, so Elizabeth held her tongue.

It felt as if she did that a very great deal, not that Mama ever realized it. She still thought Elizabeth too opinionated for a girl of just twelve years.

Perhaps that was why it was so much more pleasant to talk to dragons. They were forthright creatures with little patience for words that might obfuscate —she had just learned that word and it was fun to say in her mind—the truth. It might be best, after all, that Mama did not hear dragons. She would probably find them very, very rude.

After dinner, Mama and Jane repaired to the parlor to continue Jane's work on Mama's silhouette. One more skill Jane was very good at that Elizabeth had little interest in. Now if one could draw silhouettes of dragons, that would be far more interesting. But how would one get a tatzelwurm to hold still that long, or persuade Longbourn to sit in front of a screen? How would he even fit in the parlor? She bit her lips not to giggle.

Papa bade her come to his study with him to help him write a letter. Mama muttered something about him needing to hire a proper secretary. At least she did not insist Elizabeth come to the parlor. Something about Papa's expression suggested the letter might be something very important, indeed.

But it was all very odd, though. While she wrote a great many things for him, very important correspondence, especially with the Blue Order, he still managed to write for himself—slowly, painfully and nearly illegibly, but on his own.

He pulled the study door shut behind her and pointed her towards the small stool she usually used. Though it matched none of the other furniture in the room, it tucked neatly up under the small writing desk she wrote at so as to be out of the way.

Gracious, there was a new clutter in the room! Maps, both laid out and rolled up in carrying tubes, and some paintings of dragons that had surely not been there before, leaned against the base of the carved dragon perch that matched the dining room chairs. When had he added those to the collection?

Did he maintain the chaos because he was not a particularly tidy person, or was it because Mama detested disorder and refrained from visiting him there because of it? It was difficult to tell, and most days, both felt equally true.

He sat at his big desk, littered with piles of the detritus of his studies, and lifted his glasses. Sighing, he set them aside and scrubbed his face with his palms.

She perched on the stool and bit her tongue. Asking him what was wrong would probably not receive a direct answer anyway.

He balanced his glasses on his nose and riffled through stacks of papers on his desk, sliding them to and fro until he caught sight of the one he wanted. Did he realize three or four papers had fallen to the floor in the process? She would pick them up and return them to the desk on her way out. He plucked a folded missive from the center of a pile, a bit of blue sealing wax still clinging to the paper.

Blue sealing wax? Only the Blue Order sealed their letters that way. Why would he want to tell her what they had written?

Oh, no! It must be about April! Could they forbid their friendship? Might they insist that April leave Longbourn House? Her eyes prickled, and her face and hands turned very cold.

"As you can see, the Blue Order has written to me concerning the matters that transpired at Pembroke."

She sat very still, hands tucked under her thighs, and nodded.

"As I expected, they are not pleased." He peered over the letter and glowered at her.

Elizabeth shrank into a hunch which Mama would certainly call unattractive. Posture was most important in being considered an attractive young lady. To slouch so openly was unacceptable. But what did one do whilst anticipating something very dreadful indeed? Surely one could not be expected to sit straight and proper then—could one?

Probably. Etiquette did not seem to be a very understanding master.

"The Order is not especially fond of flitterbit fairy dragons and the problems that they bring on."

Elizabeth ground her jaws until they hurt.

"I can see you mustering your defense of them, but we will have none of that tonight. No, those creatures have alarmingly poor judgement and even poorer control of their impulses, as we see here on a daily basis." He grumbled under his breath. That was probably not in the letter, but rather a statement of his own opinion. Perhaps then, the Order did not find them so very objectionable? "They are very concerned that April has settled upon you as a Friend."

The knot in her stomach tightened until she could barely breathe. Was she really so unsuitable a companion? Miss Eva and Miss Elaine Delves were hardly more than flitterbits themselves, and they were deemed acceptable companions for fairy dragons, even though their reaction to the hatching proved them otherwise. Why would she herself not be when she did far better than they?

"You are far too young—barely twelve years old now." He drummed his fingers on the desk, slow and out of rhythm. Just a few months ago, he had been able to keep a slow, steady tapping whilst lecturing her.

Her age was hardly something she could change, but if they were just patient with her, her age would remedy itself soon enough. Certainly they could see that. If only he might vouch for her.

"The Order does not welcome members until they are at least fifteen years of age. Tending dragons is serious business and not something for children." There it was, the glare he often used to punctuate such a declaration.

She rocked back and forth, just slightly, but enough to relieve some of the building pressure in her chest. Had he forgotten? He was the one who brought her along to Pembroke in the first place. He insisted she attend the hatching to help him. That was not her fault, no more than it was her fault that April chose her as a Friend. What had he expected her to do? She clenched her fists against the hard wood of the stool seat.

"But what is done is done. Even though she is only a fairy dragon, April was duly imprinted upon humans at her hatching and is therefore governed and protected by the Blue Order. They will not take away her free choice of Friend." He wrinkled his nose and snorted. Had he learnt that habit from Longbourn? They looked rather similar when they did so. "You may begin breathing again. They will not be asking for her removal from Longbourn House."

Blood rushed back into her cheeks, leaving her a little dizzy as she sucked in a deep breath. As long as they did not forcibly wrestle her and April apart, she could tolerate anything the Order demanded.

"Under ordinary circumstances, the Order would insist you both be sent to a dedicated girls' school to be taught the ways of the Order and managed until such time as you might come out to the Order and be placed upon the Dragon Keepers' marriage mart— something you hardly need."

A school, away from home and Longbourn?

"But," something about the way he said the word was comforting and ominous at the same time. "Because I am under consideration to be named Historian of the Order, they have granted me an exception."

Historian of the Order? Papa was to be made an officer of the Order? How wonderful! If only Mama might know, she would be so proud.

When had that happened? Who had recommended him, or had he put himself forth for it? How did the Order manage such things? Was that what Sir Rowley had been talking about at Pembroke?

"They have assigned me your tutelage as the final test to my installment to that office. They have given me until the spring to teach you everything you need to know to be accepted into the Order."

Her punishment was to be taught about dragons? Surely she did not hear that correctly.

He looked at the ceiling and rolled his eyes. "I can

see what you are thinking, Lizzy. Even with all your enthusiasm, there is far more to learn than you realize."

She folded her hands tightly in her lap. "I promise, Papa, I will learn. I will be the best pupil you have ever had. I will make you proud of me." Hopefully she did not sound too pleading. He did not appreciate that tone from her.

"I know you will do your best, but you will have to apply yourself with more diligence than you realize. It will not be easy. And it is not only you. April, too, must be taught the ways of the Order and of proper behavior. She will be tested along with you."

"She is very smart and far more obliging than you realize. When I explain to her what is at stake, then I am sure she will be a very apt pupil." While Papa was right, April could be obstinate; however, she rarely determined to be so over matters of real significance. And if they disagreed on the significance, there were always extra helpings of honey that could be brought to bear to encourage her compliance.

"Do you even know what is at stake?"

"I must imagine we will not be permitted to stay at Longbourn or perhaps even stay together if we do not meet the Order's standards."

Papa grunted, eyebrows rising as though surprised. "Close enough."

"We will study very hard. The Order will find no fault with you," she whispered. She and April must not be the reason that Papa was not named Historian of the Order.

"There is something else, perhaps even as important as what you are to learn. The Order insists that you must not interact with any unfamiliar dragons until such time as you are inducted into the Order. I cannot take you on any further Order business, and you must stay away from any wild dragons—absolutely no communication with dragons you do not already know until you are granted formal permission to do so."

That was sobering indeed, but for the promise of officially joining the Order? "Yes, sir. I will do exactly as you ask."

"I expect you to mean that. Now, there is no time to waste. Help me gather the books you will need to study."

8
Chapter

January 1803

Dreary January winds whistled through a tiny gap
beside the far window in Papa's chaotic study. Despite
the fire in the fireplace, the room never really felt very
warm, which meant his joints ached, and his disposition remained decidedly sour for the entire cold season.
That was nothing new, but it did seem to be getting
worse, instead of better, no matter what the apothecary
suggested.

If only they might find a way to keep him warm during this dreadful weather. But did any place in the
house—or all of England— really feel warm during the
grey and gloomy winter months? Before April had chosen her as a Friend, Elizabeth had only given a nod to

the cold as an inevitable nuisance one endured since there was little choice. But now, she was ever aware of it, even a little afraid of it for April's sake. Tiny, cold-blooded creatures did not fare well against the ravages of a winter's day any more than Papa's temper did.

Elizabeth stood up from behind the writing desk and stretched. Hours had passed since she had last done that. She turned her back on the pile of books on the desk that threatened to topple if she jostled the desktop, or perhaps even if she sneezed. Papa's study boasted enough dust to make sneezing a very real threat.

How long had she been at her books today? Given the strident tones Mama and Papa used just outside the study door, it had probably been most of the day. Mama was not the only one who would rather see her doing something else, at least some of the time, but how else was she to learn the enormous amount Papa deemed necessary for her to meet the demands of the Order?

"I do not see why you keep Lizzy locked up amongst your books all the time. She is a girl. So much studying and reading cannot be good for her. Consider her health! Why, I just read—" Mama's strident tones pierced the heavy oak door as though it were merely paper.

"Madam, it is not your concern. Remember, I am her father—" Papa's feet shuffled, and the soft thump likely meant he was leaning heavily against the study wall, aching knees and feet probably demanding he sit down soon.

"Precisely! A daughter is of no concern to a father. She should be left to her mother's care!" How could Mama say such a thing? It seemed like the only time she took notice of Elizabeth was to find fault.

"You have Jane—and Mary, Kitty, and Lydia—all under your care. What bother is it to you to leave Lizzy to me?"

"You will leave her unfit to marry. A bluestocking of some sort whom no man will ever want. And then where will she be? She has no fortune. You would condemn her to be dependent upon her sisters?"

Elizabeth pressed her fist to her mouth and dropped back onto her stool. Mama did not think very kind things about her at all.

"Since you have not provided me with a son—" What an unusual tone of voice for Papa.

Mama's slippers scuffed along the floorboards. It was difficult to imagine her expression.

"The estate is entailed away to a young man who is destined for the clergy. I have it on good information that he is a bookish sort and motivated to please those in authority. I am preparing Lizzy to marry him."

Papa was planning for her to marry—had a husband in mind for her already? Was that supposed to be a good thing? It seemed that it should be so, but it was difficult to know.

"Marry the heir to the estate? You are preparing Lizzy to be mistress of Longbourn? But Jane—"

"How many times have you said that with Jane's beauty and sweet disposition, she will marry very well on her own merit? Without those attributes, it seems Lizzy will need a little more assistance. That is, madam, unless you can bear me a son."

Mama tittered. Was there some sort of joke that she had missed? Probably. Footfalls, two sets, wandered off toward the stairs, and the corridor became very quiet, almost distractingly so.

But it was just as well. There was a great deal more studying to be done before dinner time. How thoughtful of Mama and Papa to take their arguing elsewhere so she could try to study in quiet.

She stretched once more and returned to the pile of open books on the little writing desk.

"You have had the same pages open for quite some time." April scratched at the larger book on the desk, a great leather-bound bestiary with elaborate, though highly inaccurate, drawings of various dragons.

Elizabeth slid it aside to make room for April to perch on the blotter paper. "Have you enough room now?"

April hopped to the blotter paper. "It will do. But I do not understand why you keep staring at these same pages over and over again."

"Because they do not make any sense." Elizabeth dropped her elbows on the desk and her face into her hands. "They do not make any sense at all. I am certain that they are supposed to. If only I stare at them long enough, perhaps they will."

April stared at the page, turning her fluffy little head to and fro. "I do not see how all those scratchy lines are supposed to make any sense at all."

"Of course you do not. You are too young to learn to read."

"Your father says that fairy dragons do not read."

"Papa says a great number of things about fairy dragons, but I am not certain they all apply to you." Elizabeth scratched under April's chin.

"I am a fairy dragon."

"You are special. I have been told that there are sometimes exceptions to what is commonly understood. I think you must be one of those." That, of course, was an understatement. So far, April had managed to contradict nearly everything dragon lore had to say about fairy dragons.

Perhaps that was the reason that Papa seemed perpetually annoyed with April. He did not much like anything—or anyone—disagreeing with dragon lore.

April snorted and shook, fluffing her feather-scales out into a little blue puff. She had grown a great deal over the last several months. Not that she would ever be big; fairy dragons simply were not. But she was starting to lose a little of her baby fluffiness. She would always be cute though—fairy dragons always were. So, in at least one way, she fulfilled traditional expectations.

"So tell me why those squiggly marks are making you so upset." April pecked at the open page.

Elizabeth rubbed her eyes with the heels of her hands. "Papa has told me to read both these books and commit to memory what they say about basilisks."

"You remember things very well. Why should that bother you?"

"Remembering does not bother me, but these two books do."

"Why? You have already met a basilisk, and he was quite personable." April cocked her head and scratched her cheek, pausing a moment to clean between her toes.

"And yet this book says that basilisks do not entertain new acquaintances unless introduced formally, and only with their express permission. I am fairly certain that did not happen with Pembroke. And this one—" Elizabeth slapped the offensive page. "This one tells me never to look one in the face because its eyes will turn me to stone!"

April hopped and fluttered her wings. "That is ridiculous!"

Elizabeth squeezed her temples. "Of course it is. Yet, I am expected to memorize it and recite it as though it were true, despite the fact that if it were, I would be a statue in Miss Delves' garden." She threw her head back and stared at the dusty ceiling. "I would not mind doing so if there were some acknowledgement that this was what was once thought, and we now know better—the book was first penned two hundred years ago! One would assume that understandings might change in that amount of time. But there seems to be no accounting for new information! It is as if nothing new can be discovered about dragons—what has always been known is all that will ever be known!"

"That is silly and twitter-pated." April folded her wings back with an air of authority reminiscent of Mama settling a point.

"I agree. But how am I to discuss the matter with Papa?"

"I do not think you should. Do you recall the last time you tried …" April shivered. Even with her plucky disposition, she did not like it when Papa became cross.

"But I have to. That is the problem. What if the test I am to take asks questions about basilisks? How am I to answer when these two books do not even agree on what they look like? Just look here! It is as if they are describing two different creatures, one a snake-type dragon and one a dragon-type. If they disagree, what is the right answer to what a basilisk looks like?"

"I do not suppose you could describe Pembroke and be done with it?"

"I would, except for the fact he does not look

entirely like either description. I fear describing him would be considered absolutely wrong by any standard." She dropped her head into her hands again. "I do not know what I am going to do."

The study door swung open and Papa strode in, his step lighter than she had seen it in some time. He must have won his point with Mama.

"That does not look like studying to me." He muttered a few other things under his breath, equally grumpy, as he approached her.

Did he not realize that though Mama's hearing was not up to the task, she could hear him quite well when he did that?

"I am not wasting time, Papa. I am confused, and I do not understand what I am to make of this."

"What is there to be confused about? You are to memorize the material and repeat it when asked."

"But it does not make sense! How am I to answer questions when I do not understand?"

"What is there to understand?" He stabbed a gnarled finger at the larger book. "*Greystoke's Bestiary* lists a description of a basilisk. Memorize it."

"But it is wrong! Do you not see it? A basilisk does not resemble a dragon-type at all. And its eyes certainly do not turn anyone to stone. What is more, Blair's—"

He grabbed her by the shoulders and half-lifted her from the stool. "Do not ever, ever say such a thing again!" He shook her hard enough to leave her a little dizzy. "If I ever hear you contradict dragon lore again—"

"But the book is wrong! Pembroke—"

He shook her harder. "Never mention that, either. No one must know you have met Pembroke uninvited. What you did was tantamount to a crime."

So now she was a criminal? Because a dragon found her and talked to her? Nothing was making any sense today at all! She blinked rapidly, but her blurry vision hardly cleared. She stepped back, away from him and dragged her sleeve over her eyes. "I did not approach him; he found me. It was not my fault I was in those woods alone. I told you what the Delves sisters did."

"Never speak of that again, either. They are above you in society. You must never criticize them. You do not want to be cast in such a light. Moreover, I will not allow you to cast a shade upon Longbourn and this estate by spreading such gossip about them." When had Papa begun to care about such things? Was it Mama's influence?

"I am spreading nothing. Besides, it is not gossip when it is true."

April chittered and hopped from one foot to the other. "Do you not care that they nearly caused great harm to your daughter?"

"You should not have been foolish enough to go into the woods with them."

"And how was I to know that?"

"Because you have not been introduced to Longbourn. It is only reasonable if you do not know your own estate dragon, then you should not be meeting others."

"Did you ever teach her that?" April leaned back and hissed.

"One more word from you—"

Elizabeth threw her arm in front of April. "Do not threaten her! Do not ever threaten her! Even the Pendragon Accords say that you must not ever do such a thing!"

"Do not presume to tell me what the Accords say!"

"But you are in violation! How can you expect me to learn them properly when you do not even hold to them yourself?"

"Do not judge me, young lady. Your arrogance is appalling. I will not allow you to be an embarrassment to me or to Longbourn."

"Then simply send me away to that Blue Order school and be done with me. You will not have to worry about any association with me then. Since it seems I cannot do anything right, why do you hesitate?" Her fingers tightened into fists as she fought to catch her breath.

"You will not speak to me that way. I will not have it." He folded his arms tight across his chest and glowered with a look likely to turn her to stone.

"I just want to understand why these books say things that do not agree."

"Do not question what you do not understand."

"Then how am I to understand?'

"Just learn what Greystoke says, credit it to him, and credit Blair's statements to him. Why are you making this so difficult?"

"You did not say I had to remember what book everything came from as well."

"No more back talk, Lizzy. You are making me question the wisdom of even attempting this." He pulled off his glasses and dragged his hand down his face.

"Then do not. You have an option. Send me away and be done with it." She tucked her chin to her chest and looked away.

"I am not turning you over to some Blue Order school that will decide what you are taught, with whom you are to associate with, and whom are you to marry.

You are my daughter and my responsibility."

"One it seems you would rather not have." Except for the fact he had already decided whom she was to marry. He seemed glad enough for that.

"Enough. Go to your room immediately and do not come down for dinner. Perhaps some time for sober reflection will improve your disposition. You may stay there until you are more inclined to be agreeable and studious. Go now." He pointed a shaking hand at the door.

April launched from the desk, buzzing toward the door. Elizabeth ran behind, reaching the door just in time to open it before April flew into it. They dashed upstairs, and Elizabeth slammed the door behind her.

Why was Papa being so awful to her? If he really was so worried she would be an embarrassment to him, why would he not simply send her away?

And what would she do if he did?

Elizabeth threw herself on her bed and tried to cry. It was the right and proper thing to do at a time like this, and entirely allowable when one had been so ill-used.

Naturally, it proved well-nigh impossible. Stubborn, stubborn tears! They simply would not appear, no matter how much she wanted them to, how much better they might—at least in theory—make her feel.

Then again, all told, tears would probably upset April. She became very agitated when Lydia cried in the nursery. Seeing Elizabeth sobbing would likely send her into a frenzy that could result in pecked and bitten ears downstairs. How that would complicate matters!

What choice did she have but to bear the sick

feeling in her belly and the tightness in her chest for the time being? She drew her knees under her chin and wrapped her arms around her legs. The final rays of sunset glowed golden on the horizon, bathing her room in rich hues which promised warmth, but failed to deliver on that promise. Why did it not feel surprising that even the sun would be lying to her today?

Just how long would the disquiet last? Once she passed the Order's tests—if she passed them—would Longbourn House return to normal? Would Mama's temper cool and Papa be satisfied with her again? Or was that a thing long past since April had joined the household?

Angry voices drifted up from the base of the stairs. Mama and Papa were arguing again. Mama was insisting there were things needed for the house and her daughters that the estate could certainly afford. Papa had promised her such a life when they had married. Why was he not true to his word? If they could afford to keep Elizabeth's pet, then the other girls could certainly have what they wanted as well.

Why was it always about April? Truly, she did nothing to deserve such derision. She was less trouble than Lady Lucas' pug and never chewed up slippers. She did not yowl at the top of her lungs when visitors came like Aunt Phillips' cat. What care she needed, Elizabeth supplied, so no one in the household was put out. And she did not eat very much, even if it was nearly entirely jam and honey. If needed, Elizabeth would be happy to forgo her share of those if it meant they could better afford April's victuals. And yet, something about her presence agitated Mama.

Papa and Mama went on quarreling for some minutes, with Papa effectively unable to get a word in edgewise. Finally he shouted—sometimes the only way to silence Mama—and tried to reason with her. That rarely went well, and it certainly did not tonight. Mama's voice grew more shrill, and her logic dissolved into shrieks. Elizabeth put her fingers into her ears.

These quarrels were common enough, but still exhausting to the entire household. Jane, who could understand the words they said, would often cry half the night when they argued. Lydia, who could only pick up on the angry tones, frequently cried along with Jane, encouraging Mary and Kitty to join in just because it seemed the thing to do. Which, of course, then further upset Mama …

Perhaps it was time to step in. April had become far more adept at persuasion in the last two weeks. Maybe now was the time to put her innate talent to use on a broader scale.

She glanced at April who perched on the foot post of the bed. "Do you think you can persuade Mama to find herself content with her circumstances, at least for the moment?"

"I am not sure anyone is capable of such a thing." April twittered, cocking her head from side to side and scrunching her eyes shut. "But I will try."

Elizabeth opened her door just enough to permit April through and pressed her ear close to the opening. Scratching toes suggested April perched on the newel post at the stairs' landing, close enough that Mama might hear her persuasive voice but out of the line of sight where Mama might become more irritated by seeing her.

"You have a great many things that you want," April half-sang, half spoke, her voice so soft Elizabeth could barely make it out. "It will not hurt to wait a little while for new things."

April repeated herself several time, but Mama's words finally slowed and the shrill tones faded. That was a good sign. While she was not entirely accepting everything that April said, she was calming down, which was desirable in and of itself.

This was the first time April had so successfully persuaded Mama of anything—a milestone for her. An odd one, to be certain, but a milestone nonetheless. Apparently, persuasion was a learned skill as much as an inborn one. One more thing no one talked about in dragon lore.

Was that because Dragon Mates just knew about it or because no one bothered to write it down? Both were equally possible.

A sour taste rose in the back of her throat, and she leaned heavily against the door. Why was this all so difficult? Surely there was a missing piece that would help her to understand it all. Botheration! Sometimes Mama was every bit as vexing and contradictory as dragon lore!

April darted back in and landed on Elizabeth's shoulder as she quietly shut the door.

"He waved me off, but did not seem displeased. I shall do that more often. It is worth it to get her to stop that silly shrieking. It hurts my ears! Not everything worked, but I think I know what I shall try next time to do better. Soon, I think, I shall be able to make her very content." April preened under her wing, a very smug look on her face.

"I am sure you will be able to accomplish anything you set your mind to." Elizabeth ran a finger along April's fluffy back.

Perhaps with April's persuasion, the situation could

become more tolerable. Such a clever little creature she was.

Sunset had faded into twilight, and Elizabeth's room had grown quite dark. Given that she was banished there, she probably would not be permitted a candle. So, she crawled into bed, still dressed, and pulled the counterpane around her shoulders.

Several hours later, April nudged the side of Elizabeth's jaw. "I am hungry."

Elizabeth blinked sleep from her eyes. How long had she been asleep? It was quite dark, save a sliver of moonbeam that brightened a small path from her window to the door. The longcase clock near the base of the stairs chimed its familiar melody, ending in two distinct clangs. Her stomach rumbled in time.

Papa had said she was not to join the family for dinner. That probably also meant she was not to sneak something from the kitchen, either. She swallowed hard. It would be unpleasant, but not eating until the morning would certainly not kill her.

April, though, was another story. The cold weather made her hungry very often and missing even a single meal made her weak, sometimes too weak to fly. The Pendragon Accords were very clear: members of the Blue Order must endeavor to preserve dragon life and health under any circumstance. She had a duty to make sure April was properly fed. Even Papa could not in good conscience disagree with that.

Arguably, he should have thought of that before exiling her. Should it happen again—and realistically, there was probably a greater chance of it happening again than not—she would insist that April's needs be considered regardless of her own crimes.

She wrapped her shawl tight around her shoulders. "Tuck yourself under the folds on my shoulder, and I will take you to the kitchen."

April complied, but her movements were sluggish. She definitely needed to eat.

Elizabeth tiptoed downstairs, avoiding the two creaky steps between the first and second landings. A quick check detected no candlelight downstairs—everyone was properly in bed! She hurried to the kitchen, hopping from moonbeam to moonbeam.

A low fire glowed in the fireplace, savory warm smells coming from that side of the kitchen. Probably some sort of stew from the dinner leftovers for the house staff's breakfast. Cook had a reputation for feeding not just the family, but the servants quite well.

Along the worktable near the fireplace sat a trio of faceted glass jam pots usually placed on the breakfast table. Elizabeth lifted their lids. Each only had only a small amount left, but together they would feed a hungry fairy dragon quite nicely. She coaxed April out from under the shawl and showed her the jam.

Warmed by the fire, April quickly hopped to her favorite strawberry jam pot to begin her repast before Elizabeth could spoon out the jam into a proper dish. April's manners still left something to be desired, so Elizabeth turned her back and wandered deeper into the kitchen. Now was not the time for teaching niceties to a ravenous dragon—even if it was only a fairy dragon.

How loudly April guzzled and slurped her meal. Exactly what Elizabeth imagined a large dragon would sound like when devouring its prey. Odd, how easily people forgot the essential dragon-nature of fairy dragons. They were adorable, and fluffy, and sometimes a bit addle-pated, but they were still dragons, with the predatory instincts, territorial tendencies, and the pride inherent to the dragon nature. Papa himself often seemed to forget that April was fully a dragon. Would he be so dismissive if she looked more like Rustle, Uncle Gardiner's very imposing-looking cockatrice? Somehow that was hard to picture. Dangerous-looking creatures seemed far more difficult to ignore. Perhaps that was why they garnered more respect.

In the dim firelight, the kitchen seemed a very dreary place. It probably was in the daylight, too. Everything was utilitarian and crammed together in what felt like not enough space. Although there were windows, they seemed hardly large enough to bring in enough light to work, especially in the early morning hours when Cook began her day. No wonder she always seemed cross. Perhaps it was not such a bad thing that Mama did not want her daughters in the kitchen.

How odd—wait, what was that sound? Scratching? Scraping? Thumping? It seemed vaguely familiar, but from where? The noises were louder near the cellar door. She crept toward it. Yes, they were definitely growing louder. She pressed her ear to the cold, coarse door. Whatever was making those sounds was in the cellar below.

She hurried to find a candle and lit it in the fireplace.

April pulled her head up from the pot of blackberry preserves. "Where are you going?"

"I want to see what is making noise in the cellar."

"I do not think you should go downstairs. Your mother says you should not even be in the kitchen, and your father said—"

"He told me to stay away from unknown dragons. There cannot possibly be an unknown dragon in the cellar. That is just silly."

"I am still hungry."

"I did not tell you to leave your meal. Finish eating. You know where I will be."

April harrumphed and returned to her preserves.

Elizabeth pulled the cellar door open far enough that she could slip inside. It took a few moments for her eyes to adjust to the deeper darkness of the cellar. With no windows to capture even the faint moonlight, the candle offered the only glow to penetrate the blackness.

The stairs were narrow and irregular and creaky. Cobwebs, complete with a few large spiders, dangled from the walls and the crossbeams that held the floor above her. Cool, dank air that smelt of stone and stale water urged her to pull her shawl tighter.

"Bennet?" The voice was deep and rumbly, grouchy, and very familiar.

"Longbourn?" Elizabeth peered into the depths of the cellar as a scaly green head came closer.

"What are you doing here?" they asked simultaneously.

"This is my territory. Why should I not be here?" Longbourn grumbled, drumming his foot on the dirt floor.

"And this is my house. Why should I not be here?" Even in her own ears, she sounded short and irritated.

"You ae not permitted in the cellar."

Why did he have to sound like her father just now? "How would you know that?"

He leaned close to her face and snorted softly.

She matched his posture, until her nose nearly touched his. "Why did you come to the house?"

"My Keeper and I needed to talk." Something in

Longbourn's voice was unsettling. Clearly he was not happy, but there was something more. Angry, maybe? But even that did not capture it.

"Oh," she looked over her shoulder. "I should go then." She retreated back a step. It was one thing when Papa sounded angry, but a dragon was entirely another.

"Do not leave. Why would you leave?" Longbourn pulled back and turned his head nearly sideways.

"I do not think Papa would want me to be here." Blast and botheration, her voice quivered just when she did not want it to.

"Something is wrong. What is wrong?"

"Nothing. Nothing that is worth worrying a dragon for." She turned her face away from him—his peering into her eyes was just too intense.

"Where is the blue fluffletuft? You are never without her."

"In the kitchen, eating."

Longbourn grumbled deep in his throat. "Why would she be hungry in the middle of the night?"

Elizabeth pressed her fist to her mouth and huddled in on herself.

Longbourn sniffed her up and down, snuffling and muttering under his breath. Gently—for a creature his size—he nudged her down the stairs. He sat on his haunches several strides from the base of the stairs and urged her close enough to wrap his wing around her. "Tell me."

Why those simple words and a cold scaly embrace should rend the tears from her now made little sense. But they did. It was a wonder he could understand her stammering, sobbing explanations as she poured out her frustrations to him.

He pulled her tight into his side and held her there

until the tears finally receded into soft hiccoughs. She rubbed her face with her sleeve. "I know I am just being silly and stupid."

"Silly is a warm-blooded notion that I neither know nor care for. But stupid you are not, not at all. I will not tolerate you being made to feel so." He thumped his tail in a peculiar but intentional seeming rhythm against the floor.

"What are you doing?"

"Calling your father."

"Pray, no do not! He will be ever so angry—"

The door at the top of the stairs flew open, banging against the wall. "What is it now? Have you another demand I cannot meet?" Papa held a small candle near his face. Flickering shadows made his wide eyes wild-looking. "Elizabeth!"

She huddled against Longbourn. If only she could have hidden behind his wing and avoided detection altogether.

"What in Pendragon's name are you doing here? I told you the Order required you to stay away from all unfamiliar dragons! How dare you disobey a direct—"

Longbourn slowly stood, growling. "I am not an unfamiliar dragon."

"I have never presented her to you."

"I did not need you to. I met her when she was out walking, and we became introduced." Longbourn nodded at her, pulling her a little closer.

"Elizabeth! How could you—"

"She did nothing inappropriate—unless you consider not screaming and running away inappropriate behavior." Longbourn pulled his lips back, not quite into a snarl.

"It is what most girls would do under the

circumstances."

"She is not most girls."

"Apparently so." Papa pinched the bridge of his nose and stared into Elizabeth's face. "That does not change the fact that you have not been made ready to make an acquaintance with major dragons!"

Longbourn thumped his tail a little harder. "We do not share your warm-blooded notion of being 'out' in society or not."

"She has not learned proper etiquette—"

"She understands far more than most full Dragon Keepers and is ready and willing to learn more. I have been tutoring her—"

Papa slapped his forehead and huffed. "You, tutoring my daughter? That is absurd. Major dragons do not—"

Longbourn smacked his tail hard on the cellar floor. Dust and cobwebs fell from the floorboards above them. "It is not for you to say. We will interact with those we find worthy. Your daughter is worth her salt. I will vouch for her before the Order."

Papa's expression changed, abruptly and dramatically. "Worth her salt, you say?"

What was that in Papa's tone? The change was unmistakable, but what did it mean?

Elizabeth felt as much as heard Longbourn's rumble. "That is what I said."

Papa descended the stairs quickly, nearly tripping on the last two.

"Elizabeth, collect April and return to your room. You may take the jam pot with you if she has not finished. There is some bread left from dinner on the table near the jam. Get yourself some, perhaps cheese, as well. Go."

Longbourn urged her up and steadied her until her knees felt solid again. She dashed up the stairs, skirting around Papa, and into the kitchen.

It took only a moment to wrap a bit of bread and cheese in a napkin, take up the jam pot, and scurry upstairs, April buzzing wildly to keep up.

9
Chapter

Well-sated on jam, April quickly fell asleep, cuddled between Elizabeth's neck and shoulder, tucked under the counterpane to ensure she did not take a chill. With Elizabeth's own belly no longer rumbling, she fought to lie still and not disturb April.

Swiftly moving thin clouds, carried on cold breezes, made the moonlight dance along the floorboards and across the bed. The eerie, angular shapes seemed entirely fitting for the very peculiar events of the evening. She huddled a little deeper into the feather bed.

What an odd, odd conversation that had been. Longbourn's unwavering support—heavens! She bit her knuckle lest she lend voice to her astonishment. Finding him in the cellar to begin with had been quite a surprise! A welcome one, to be sure, but entirely surprising.

How unusual that he should take her side in a

quibble with Papa. He was Keeper. Should not his opinions take precedence? Then again, it was strange that Longbourn would take notice of her, a child—a girl child—in the first place.

What were he and Papa talking about in the cellar? She shifted under the covers. If only she dared creep downstairs and listen in. But it was one thing to listen when one could not avoid it. Eavesdropping intentionally was an entirely different matter; it simply was not done. She would have to wait until someone saw fit to tell her. Uneasy thoughts turned over and over in her mind until she finally fell asleep.

Not long after sunrise, strident voices roused Elizabeth from a deep sleep. Mama and Papa, fighting, again? She pulled the counterpane over her head, but it did little to dampen the sound. It was early, very early for that. Should not April's persuasions have had a longer effect?

"Of course Jane should come out when she turns fifteen. How can you possibly think otherwise?" Mama's pitch climbed steadily higher. Soon it would match April's and be impossible for any but dragon-hearing folk to detect.

"Fifteen is entirely too young for Jane or any of the other girls to be out."

"I think that is my decision, not yours, Mr. Bennet." Mama's heel came down hard on the floor. Was she trying to inflame Papa's temper?

"I do not know what has possessed you, madam, but I am certainly *involved* in such a decision."

"It is a mother's business to know when her daughters should be out. I declare that fifteen is a fitting age for our Jane. I was out at fifteen if you remember."

"I am entirely aware of that." Papa probably clapped his hand over his eyes. "Jane would be much better off waiting."

"But her sisters will not."

"Whatever do you mean?" That was Papa's truly puzzled voice.

"We have five daughters to marry, Mr. Bennet! Five daughters!" Was that Mama smacking the back of her hand into her other palm? "If we wait too long for Jane to be out, then all the girls will have to wait. Lydia might well be a spinster before she even has the opportunity to come out."

"You are exaggerating."

"Hardly. Look at the Lucases. Their oldest girl, Charlotte, she is out now—almost twenty she is and how much interest has there been in her? Almost none, I tell you. It is a good thing her younger sisters are far younger than she. Otherwise, they would be growing stale waiting for Charlotte to find a match, if she ever does. Do not forget, there is a shortage of marriageable young men, especially here in the country. Now, perhaps if we were to go to London—"

"Have you not always said the Lucas girl was plain and ordinary, without fortune or anything to set her apart? Perhaps that might be part of the issue?"

"Have you forgotten how little our girls have—unless you have managed to set any more aside for them?"

Elizabeth cringed. Mama and Papa had argued over that very issue several times a month for as long as she could remember. The first argument she had overheard between them was about Papa not fulfilling his promise to add to their dowries.

"I have already explained to you—I have the

situation well in hand. You need not worry for yourself or the girls—" Papa was trying to sound patient, but he did not do it well.

"There is no assurance that things will play out as you describe. No assurance at all! Good intentions do not always ensure good outcomes. The current heir to Longbourn might not even live long enough to take over. Then where will this plan of yours be? Influenza is known to kill young men as well as old. And the possibility of accidents on horseback, or fires; he might fall down a set of stairs—"

"You could always provide a son, as you assured me you would when we married." Why did he have to say that?

Mama shrieked and cried out in words that Elizabeth could neither understand nor cared to. She plugged her ears with her fingers until the din moved away—probably to some other part of the house.

Despite the sick feeling in her stomach, she drifted back to sleep with the help of April's sweet song.

Shortly after the longcase clock chimed eight times, Mama burst into Elizabeth's room, clapping sharply. "Up, up, now is not the time to be a lay-abed. Get dressed as quickly as you can. Hill will be here in a few minutes to help you pack."

"Pack?" Elizabeth sat up and rubbed her eyes with her fists. Gracious, the sun was very bright this morning!

"Yes, I said pack. I—I have business in London that cannot wait another day, not another moment. You and your sisters are coming with me."

"Why?" The words slipped out before she could hold them back.

"Do not question me, Miss Elizabeth. Just because your father thinks your future is settled, does not mean you are any safer than your sisters are. I will not have you holding that over them."

Elizabeth's forehead wrinkled. What was Mama going on about?

"Do not play games with me. You know what your father is about, and he has you convinced that everything will work according to his plan. I can tell you with great assurance; plans do not always work out as they should. Things happen, unexpected things, things that can leave a family in dire straits. I have seen it happen too many times. I do not intend to see that happen to my girls. I will do everything in my power to see you properly situated so that you shall never want. Mark my words; I shall do it."

Elizabeth cocked her head and blinked, drawing a deep breath. Was any of this supposed to make sense?

"No more questions! My head! My nerves! Just do as I said, and get dressed. Hill will be with you shortly." Mama trundled out, flustered and bustling like an angry hen.

She probably would not appreciate the comparison.

Before Elizabeth had time to ponder further, Hill dragged a half-packed trunk into her room. A peek confirmed that Jane's things already took up the bottom half of the trunk. Hill helped her to finish dressing and turned to packing with barely a word.

That was probably more disturbing than Mama's agitation. Hill always had a pleasant word and engaging small talk to share with whomever was near. Mama found it too familiar, but Elizabeth enjoyed it and always found it instructive in one manner or another. Without it, the room seemed colder than it was, and her stomach ached.

Less than an hour later, Elizabeth had eaten a few bites of breakfast and stood outside the front door, waiting for the family coach, April burrowed deep in the depths of her cloak's hood. Mama would probably not want her to come, but leaving her behind was not an option.

The sharp breeze from last night continued to bully thin clouds across the bright sky. The day would be cold and crisp—and very, very strange. Whispers between the maids, ones that they did not intend for her to hear, revealed that Papa had left in quite a temper less than two hours ago. He said something about business that would keep him out all day. The maids were certain that the business would likely be finding some accommodating pub in which to drown his sorrows. Papa hardly ever went out, much less for an entire day. This was serious, indeed.

The driver pulled the carriage to the front door, and Mama ushered them into the coach, like a mama duck with her ducklings. She sat across from Elizabeth, with Jane and Lydia at her sides. The thin squabs seemed harder than usual, and the coach more confined than it had ever been. Kitty and Mary pressed close to Elizabeth. Her sisters' expressions ranged from puzzled to frightened to decidedly miserable. Unlike Elizabeth, they had little experience traveling and had no idea what to expect.

"Where are we going, Mama?" Jane asked as Longbourn House disappeared from the side glass.

"To London, to see your Uncle Gardiner. He is a good brother and will see everything is made right. Everything will be made right, I assure you, girls. You have nothing to worry about." Mama put her arms around Lydia and Jane, but nothing in her expression said anything would ever be all right again.

Jane's eyes filled with tears, but she managed, somehow, to hold them back, which was good, because if she cried, Lydia and Mary would surely follow. Then this journey would move from uncomfortable to unbearable.

If only there were a way for April to sing a bit and calm everyone down, but she could hardly do that without drawing notice to herself, so they would have to do without her assistance. As if this journey were not already difficult enough. Elizabeth bit her lip. Nothing she could possibly say would be useful at this moment.

Three very long hours later, the coach crossed into London proper. Many of the sights and sounds as they had passed through in the streets were fascinating, but the dragons were even more so. Wild dragons in the air—or at least they seemed wild, perched on the corners of buildings like falcons waiting to catch unsuspecting pigeons. Several small drakes that surely passed as terriers scampered in the streets, after rats, no doubt. Children played nearby, seemingly unaware of their unusual company.

Perhaps she might—no, she could not. Papa had been ever so stern with her. She was not permitted to meet new dragons right now. She swallowed back the lump in her throat. At least there was Rustle, the cockatrice, at Uncle Gardiner's house. He was a bit grumpy at times, but grumpy dragon company was far better than none at all.

The carriage pulled into the mews behind Uncle Gardiner's Cheapside home. Elizabeth had never been to London, but the mews looked quite like they did in other places: rather closed in, useful, but not very attractive. A number of the houses had small gardens in the mews, which was little different to the smaller cities she had been to with Papa, but she probably should not comment on that. Mama did not like to be reminded that Elizabeth had experiences which her sisters had not.

The driver climbed down from the box and meandered to the door. It must have taken a quarter of an hour for the door to open again and Uncle Gardiner to hurry out to them.

He pulled the carriage door open and leaned inside. "Fanny? My dear sister, where is Thomas? Whatever has brought you all this way so unexpectedly?"

"Please, Edward, may we stay with you?" Mama folded her hands together and batted her eyes, but real dread colored her voice.

"Of course, you know you always have a place with me. But pray tell me, where is Thomas?" He reached to help her out.

"I will tell you everything, but first, permit me to settle the girls. They are not used to traveling and must rest." Mama stepped down from the coach and beckoned them to follow.

With the help of Uncle's housekeeper, Mama ushered them upstairs, to an attic room clearly intended as a nursery. The maid rushed to remove the dust cloths from the furniture, revealing two little beds and one larger, lined up against the longest wall. Tall, narrow windows brought light into the white painted room, enough that it did not feel too dreary. A doll, a wooden horse, and a pair of hoops lay in the corner near a large leather-wrapped trunk which probably contained more toys. Next to it a small shelf held a few books—baby books, nothing that Elizabeth would want to read, but they might keep Kitty and Lydia entertained.

Elizabeth bit her tongue at the indignity of being consigned to a nursery. She might not be out, but it had been years since she had to keep to the nursery. The housekeeper, dear soul that she was, managed to whisper that a guest room would be made up for her and Jane later. In the meantime, though, she was expected to nap quietly whilst sharing a bed with Jane and Mary—and April, who did not much like the close proximity.

Her sisters fell asleep in very short order, but Elizabeth's mind raced too fast to allow her to rest. What would Longbourn think about her removal from the estate? What would happen to April whilst they were here? With so many predators about, she could hardly go out on her own. Did Uncle even know she had brought a fairy dragon into his home?

And what about Rustle? In the wild, cockatrice ate fairy dragons. Introducing predator to prey and expecting them to be friendly was a skill she had not even read about, much less learnt.

What if Mama did not wish to return to Longbourn? What would they do here in London? Could Papa force them to move back? Legally he had that right, but would he exercise it? And if he did, what would it mean for things at home? Surely, it would not improve Mama's disposition.

Elizabeth slipped out of bed, slowly and carefully enough not to disturb Jane and Mary, and tiptoed to the little wooden bench near the windows. She curled up on the hard seat in the path of a wan sunbeam, drawing her knees under her chin.

How could she feel so alone in a room so full of her

sisters? Shrill tones—her mother's, no doubt—drifted up from the floors below. She was too far away to make out what Mama was saying, but the pitch and cadence was enough to suggest a very great deal. How was Uncle to manage her?

Her sisters woke two hours later. The housekeeper arrived very shortly thereafter with a dinner tray and an announcement that Jane and Elizabeth would be moving to another room. Mary, Kitty, and Lydia seemed pleased they would have the entire nursery to themselves.

The housekeeper stayed with them through dinner and, with the help of a maid, established Jane and Elizabeth in a downstairs bedroom already containing their trunk. The room was smaller than Elizabeth's room at home and faced the mews. That was nice since the street noises would not keep them awake. The large bed looked thick and fluffy and inviting, far more comfortable than the one in the nursery. The pale wood furniture might be a little old and plain by Mama's standards, but it was tidy and comfortable and welcoming.

Mama visited them shortly thereafter, speaking many words, but with very little substance in any of them. She seemed to be a little calmer, though, and that had to be a good thing.

Jane retrieved her work bag from the trunk and pulled a chair near the window. Why she found fancy sewing so soothing, Elizabeth hardly understood, but it was good to see her smile just a little.

"Do not worry, Lizzy. I am sure it will all work out for the best. I think it is nice to visit London. I have never been away from Meryton before."

Elizabeth murmured something agreeable

sounding. Jane never liked to talk about anything unpleasant, which was probably just as well. It was not as if there was very much either of them could do to affect the situation.

Bedtime came, and Jane fell asleep directly—how did she do that?

Elizabeth scrunched her pillow, trying to get comfortable.

April poked her ear with sharp little toes. "I am hungry."

Of course she was, and she had every right to be so. But this was not Longbourn.

"I must introduce you to Rustle before I dare poke about the kitchen. This is his territory, after all. Come, I will see if I can find him." Elizabeth wrapped her dressing gown around herself and tiptoed toward the stairs.

Where would Rustle be? The most likely place would be Uncle's study, but Mama's voice still drifted up from that direction. Since Rustle did not hide his dislike of Mama, he would certainly not stay in the room with her. Hopefully, he would not be in Uncle's chambers. She would not be able to talk to him there.

"You are supposed to be in bed."

She jumped and looked up.

Rustle peered down at her from the top of the parlor door. His long taloned toes gripped the door, and his wings were extended. He was trying to look big. "Go back to bed."

A shiver coursed down her back. But he intended that, no doubt. Unlike fairy dragon voices which were soothing and soporific, cockatrice voices induced terror when properly applied.

"Pray forgive my intrusion, but—may we go into

the parlor?" She glanced into the room, lit only by moonlight.

Rustle offered a patronizing look but swooped into the parlor. "What have you to tell me?" He landed on the back of the largest chair in the room, near the windows. His serpentine tail snaked along the upholstery, helping him balance.

"I am sorry to impose upon your hospitality, uninvited, especially with one whom you have never made acquaintance with. Pray, may I introduce you to my Dragon Friend?" She covered April with her hand lest she make a sudden move that triggered Rustle's prey instincts.

Rustle sniffed the air. "I thought I smelt another dragon about. A fairy dragon? It smells like fruit."

"Yes, she is still very young and could not stay behind when Mama packed us up."

Rustle flapped and grumbled and snorted. Small dragons did not like to share territory any more than large ones. "Very well, it seems we have little alternative. You would, no doubt, go into the street with her if I said no."

"Indeed, I would, though, I am sure that would only upset Mama further."

Rustle growled and snapped his sharp beak. "Show me this fairy dragon."

Elizabeth lifted her hand, and April peeked out from under the dressing gown collar. "May I present April, my Dragon Friend. This is Rustle, Friend to my Uncle Gardiner. He is a very fine cockatrice, a powerful protector to this home." A little sincere flattery was rarely lost upon a minor dragon.

April covered her head with her wings and pressed herself nearly flat on Elizabeth's shoulder. "I am honored to make your acquaintance."

Rustle leaned close and sniffed her. His long forked tongue snaked out, and he licked the top of her head. "I admit you into my territory."

"Thank you." April peeked out between her wings. She was not normally so docile, but perhaps knowing she might easily be a late night snack shaped her manners.

"Her voice is weak. Did the housekeeper bring her dinner with yours?" His beak clapped in a cockatrice equivalent of a frown.

"No, it seems she does not believe that children should have jam with their bread or honey with their tea."

"I see. Wait here." Rustle flapped away.

A few minutes later he returned, carrying a jam pot in his talons. "Here." He dropped it, clattering, on the table in front of Elizabeth. "Eat. Hungry dragons are not pleasing company for anyone. I will see that my guest has suitable victuals in the future."

He really was a thoughtful, charming creature ... for a dragon.

"That is very kind of you." Elizabeth opened the pot, and April dove for it, muttering "thank you" through mouthfuls.

"Does the Order know you are here?"

"I do not think so. We did not even know we were coming until we left."

"They should. It is important." Rustle paced along the edge of the chair. "Pray excuse me." He flew off before she could object.

Hopefully, the Order did not make things more complicated. But that seemed highly unlikely.

She yawned and stretched. April must really like the

jam Rustle brought; she had stopped guzzling and now seemed to savor each bite. Elizabeth sat on the sofa near the table. Perhaps it would not hurt to close her eyes a bit as she waited for April to finish.

"Rustle told me I would find you here." Uncle whispered, standing over her. "No, no need to answer, there is no trouble. Let me take you up to bed, though. Your mother would be most vexed to find you out of your room." He picked her up and carried her back to the guest room, April quietly following.

The next morning, a maid roused Jane and Elizabeth, helped them dress, and escorted them down to the morning room where Mama and Uncle Gardiner already waited. It was odd being woken for the day. At Longbourn, Elizabeth was usually the first one of the family up and about.

The morning room was smaller than Longbourn's morning room, but yellow paper hangings with white birds made it warm and cheerful. Mama said all those homey touches could be attributed to her dear and departed mother who was the last mistress of that house. A house was never a home, she said, without a woman to manage it. She had offered a few speculations about how the new Mrs. Gardiner might fare when she was elevated to mistress of the house, but those musings were often less than charitable, so it did not serve to dwell on them.

The table was set with a tempting variety of dishes, offering a wealth of appetizing scents as they walked in, a very effective way of reminding one that she was hungry.

April caught sight of a pot of jam set very near one seat and hummed in Elizabeth's ear. Uncle Gardiner gestured Elizabeth toward that chair. April twittered her gratitude and hopped down on the table.

Mama slapped the table, sending April hovering above the tabletop. "Elizabeth! How many times have I told you? Your pet is not welcome at the table! Oh, Brother, pray forgive her. I cannot see why she brought that creature with us to London in the first place. If I had only known, I would surely—"

Rustle swooped in to perch on the back of Uncle Gardiner's chair and chirruped at Mama. It was not a friendly sound.

Mama glared at Rustle, eyes wide and even a mite offended.

"Pray be at ease, Fanny. Truly, it is of no concern to me." Uncle looked over his shoulder at Rustle, a little reproach in his expression. "You see Rustle has free reign of the house. His table manners are as refined as most of my guests'."

Elizabeth sniggered only for Mama to glower at her. On the far side of the table, Jane made herself as small as possible. She hated conflict.

"I insist. Elizabeth, take that creature out of the morning room before it and Uncle's bird start to peck at each other as the chickens do."

Uncle shook his head. "Rustle and April seem to be on quite friendly terms, so I cannot see any point in banishing the little creature to the guest rooms."

"Sometimes you sound just like Mr. Bennet. I cannot say I like it at all. I am sure it is that club—Blue's is it?—that you both belong to. Who has heard of that place? It seems to foster very strange preferences and ideas."

Uncle cleared his throat rather loudly. "I would thank you to not comment on business that is no concern of yours."

Mama's eyes bulged, and she sucked in a sharp breath. Papa was not apt to make such pointed remarks, but considering the way it ended that line of conversation, perhaps he should.

"I had thought, though," Uncle turned and looked at Elizabeth with a particular intensity that strongly suggested she should agree to whatever he said, "that perhaps little April might find it comfortable to have a place of her own to retreat to when tired. It might be wrapped up warmly to keep her from the chill in the winter and to protect her from undesired company when she might prefer a bit of privacy."

"Privacy, for a bird? Really, Edward, you are indulging Elizabeth's fantasies far too much. They are already quite out of control."

April pulled her face from the jam pot and twittered. "I rather fancy the notion."

"Hear how prettily she is singing? She likes the idea." Uncle winked at April.

Mama harrumphed. "Oh, very well. If it will keep that creature contained, then perhaps it is a good idea."

Elizabeth bit her lip. "You do not mean a—"

Uncle cut her off with a glance. "I think you shall be very pleased with what I propose. After breakfast, I shall take you and April on a little outing to see what I have in mind."

"I am sure Jane would like very much to go with you as well." Mama looked suggestively at Jane.

Jane's eyebrows lifted just a mite.

"No, you would not." Rustle and April said simultaneously.

"You would much rather stay here and entertain Kitty and Lydia. They need to have someone familiar nearby. London is such a strange place and so far from home for them." April added with authority.

Jane's brows knit and creased her forehead "Kitty and Lydia were so restless last night. I think it would be better for me to stay and entertain them."

Mama's face flushed, and she opened her mouth to speak.

"It is a mark of the sweetness of Jane's disposition that she should be willing to forego her own pleasures for the sake of her younger sisters." April cheeped.

"You are such a sweet girl. How can I deny you such a request?" Mama looked almost surprised at the words which tumbled from her mouth.

"It is settled then. Finish up your breakfast, and I will see you in my study, Lizzy." Uncle nodded and excused himself from the table.

Elizabeth ate quickly, almost as hastily as April who seemed to want to be away from Mama's company as fast as possible.

Mama waved her out of the room. "Go quickly now, to your Uncle, and do not be a bother to him. He is not used to all the prattle and questions little girls are apt to be about."

Rustle followed them to Uncle's study.

"Are you ready then? Shall we be off?" Uncle held out her cloak and bonnet.

April took her place in the folds of Elizabeth's hood as they stepped out into the crisp morning air. Rustle followed, flying low overhead, silhouetted against the bright, cloudless sky.

"Where are we going?" Elizabeth glanced up at Uncle Gardiner.

He took her hand, smiling. "You need not worry. We are going to the Blue Order."

"Are there not dragons there?" She gasped, her feet freezing in place. "I am not supposed to meet any new ones, not yet, not now."

"I understand the restrictions you are under. But Rustle has already been there. Permission has been extended for you to visit. And yes, should your father need to know about it, I will make sure he understands the permissions granted you."

She squeezed his hand, her throat too tight to speak. The Blue Order! She was going to finally see the Blue Order! Who could have thought such a wondrous thing might happen on a trip such as this one! Papa had described the place, and made it sound rather dull and mundane. Somehow it did not seem possible she could agree with such an assessment, not when there would be so many dragons there.

In what felt like a very few minutes, they stopped before a rather plain white building, five stories tall. Fine iron railings danced before its many windows, none of which she could see into. Large double doors, painted the Order's signature blue, stood sentinel before them. The effect was a bit disappointing. Such a marvelous place should have stood out, been grand and impossible to miss, rather than blending into the surroundings. Then again, that was what dragons did too, blending in and hiding in plain sight.

Maybe it was fitting that the Blue Order offices did the same.

Papa had once said what made the offices truly impressive were the labyrinth of tunnels underneath the building. Multiple levels of cellars had been dug out, extending the office farther underground than it was above. From the offices, a myriad of tunnels ran under the whole of London, connecting many of the great structures and houses to the Great Court and Hall of the Blue Order on the deepest subterranean level.

The Great Court was said to host all manner of Order events, both social and judicial. It was the one place where major dragons and Keepers could come together in large numbers with the dragon-deaf populace left none the wiser. If only she might get to see it someday.

Uncle Gardiner rapped at the door. A somber, blue-coated servant opened the door. Uncle presented his signet, the one all Blue Order members had, and they were admitted into a huge entry hall. White marble with veins of grey and gold lined the floor and the grand, sweeping staircase about twenty paces ahead. An oak railing, carved in the form of large wyrms, flanked the stairs. A minor dragon graced each spindle, but they were too far away to make out the fine details. April peeked out from her hood to look.

A blue-liveried footman met them and inquired after their business. Uncle explained, and the footman offered direction to his destination. "The little girl and her Friend should wait for you in the parlor."

"I will escort her and chaperone her for the duration," Rustle squawked.

"Very well." The footman gestured for Elizabeth to follow Rustle. With Uncle's nod, she obeyed.

He flew to the staircase and upstairs, almost too fast for her to keep up with him and certainly too fast for her to actually admire the carvings. How unfair! Worse still, it probably was not proper to run up the stairs, but if she lost track of him, how would she ever find her way in a place so vast? April barely managed to keep her grip on Elizabeth's shoulder. Pray she did not fall off, lest they become totally disconnected from Rustle. Thankfully, he waited for her at the first landing.

"The parlor is not far. This way." He pointed down the corridor with his wing and launched.

At least in the corridor, she only had to walk briskly, not run, to keep up. It still earned her a few stern glares from cranky-looking old men as she made her way to a very large, open door—one large enough that Longbourn, if he ducked, could pass through. A building designed for dragons! A chill snaked down her spine. Was there ever a place so wonderful?

She peeked into the room. The huge expanse seemed less a parlor and more a fantastical reading room, populated equally by humans and dragons. Windows covered the far wall. Light poured in through glass that seemed covered with a light coating of frost. No wonder she had not been able to see inside from the street. What a clever way to prevent accidental glimpses of those within.

The wall adjacent to the windows boasted bookcases extending to the ceiling, shelves loaded with tomes of every shape and size, some bowing under the weight. Opposite the windows, curiosities abounded. Shelves, cases, sideboards all bore so many wonderful things. Framed feathers and scales, teeth and claws, carvings of creatures familiar and not. If only she might look at them all! April cheeped and shuddered, pointing at several of the artifacts—no doubt reminders of the predatory dragons which plagued her kind.

Tables and chairs, some near the windows, and others in clusters around card tables, filled the center of the room. Men played cards. A pair of drakes seemed to be playing draughts next to a trio of cockatrice playing at some kind of table top bowling that involved kicking a ball to and fro.

How unexpected. But then of course, it only made sense that dragons would have special games that they played just as men did.

"You are staring," Rustle whispered in her ear.

"Pray excuse me." She turned her gaze to the floor. Did dragons mind being stared at as people did? Papa had never mentioned.

Rustle led her to an overstuffed leather chair near the window, several books piled on the nearby pedestal table—a magnificent lindwurm, covered in ormolu, supported the round marble tabletop! "I am sure you can occupy yourself quite contentedly whilst you wait. I have some business to conduct. Stay here until I return for you."

Had he not said he would chaperone her? But if she said something, would she sound ungrateful for this opportunity and be asked to leave? Best not to take the chance. She climbed into the chair and pulled the stack of books into her lap.

The topmost book boasted a magnificent green leather binding, tooled in a dragon scale pattern and edged in gold. *The Society of Drakes: The Rules and Order Found in a Congenial Community of Minor Dragons Unremarked upon Elsewhere.* Her heart beat a little faster. Minor drakes lived together? Was that possible? Dragon lore considered dragons solitary creatures who did not form communities.

She licked her lips and opened to the first chapter: *The establishment of dominance in the social hierarchy.* The author seemed terribly fond of using very long words, and as many phrases in Latin as he could fit in. That was a shame as it made the text very difficult to read.

Perhaps Papa would allow her to learn Latin at some point—if only to make it easier for her to read dragon lore. Surely that would be a sufficient reason to justify teaching it to a girl.

April hopped to the chair's arm to stare at the illustrations in the text, cocking her head to and fro as though she could read along. Maybe someday.

Even without those words she could not understand, the chapter was fascinating. This new information, together with what Longbourn had told her, made the concepts about dominance among dragons make so much sense! Of course, it was so obvious! How could she have missed the profound importance of what it took to establish territory in creating a pecking order among drakes!

"Tsk, tsk, tsk."

She jumped and looked over her shoulder.

A slate-grey drake with sharp spine ridges stood on his hind legs close behind her and peered at the page she read. "The author has the basic notions correct, but I fear he oversimplified matters."

"Indeed? In what way?" She turned to face him.

He beckoned to a blue-grey drake with a pair of short horns. "Come, help me explain, Cloudy. You too, Mist and Thunder." A pair of pale grey, hooded drakes looked at him.

A moment later she was surrounded by four drakes, standing on their back legs, rendering them just about her height. April hopped back into her hiding place in Elizabeth's hood. Without introductions, the group of drakes must have been very intimidating.

"Ah yes," Mist leaned over the arm of the chair and peered at the book. "A very good, basic text on the subject, if a bit simplified. He misses some of the finer nuances of the matter." She turned to Thunder. "If you will assist me?"

He nodded, dropping to all fours and turning his barrel chest toward Elizabeth.

The four drakes patiently demonstrated what the book had tried to describe, pointing out the finer details that had been glossed over, which, at least in this case, seemed to make all the difference. With their encouragement, she joined in the exercise, using her cloak to stand in for a frilled hood and the ability to puff herself up to larger proportions.

Mist and Cloudy, the smallest of the group, ducked under and around her cape, sniffing and ruffling it.

"Very clever, very clever, indeed. The use of such a garment would make communication much clearer under so many circumstances." Mist turned over her shoulder and flared her hood open and closed whilst waving her tail.

A very large, very blue snake slithered from the darkest corner of the room directly toward them. What a spectacular noise it made as it went, like a company of men marching. A blue pa snake! Gracious, she had never seen one before, much less met one. What had that book on introductions said about snake-type greetings?

The pa snake stopped in front of her and lifted head and shoulders until he "stood" about Uncle Gardiner's height. His eyes glittered like jet beads as his dainty tongue tasted the air.

Elizabeth dropped to her knees and pulled her cloak over her head. "I am honored to make your acquaintance."

"I am Castordale. My territory's Keeper is Sir Edward Dressler. Who are you?"

She peeked up. "Miss Elizabeth Bennet. My father is Keeper to Longbourn."

Castordale flicked the back of her head with his tongue, and she slowly rose.

"She has been reading on drake society." Mist bobbed her head slightly.

Castordale's tail curled around behind him, and he sat back on it. "One of my favorite courses of study. Go on."

The drakes began talking over one another with points they wished Castordale to explain and gestures they wished her to demonstrate with her cloak. He seemed only too happy for the society and launched into detailed, if occasionally confusing, explanations. His response to her cloak was entirely unexpected. He declared it exceptionally clever for a warm-blood, deserving of a monograph! Papa would never believe it!

Somewhere amidst the animated conversation, two footmen appeared bearing a tea service. Castordale urged her to partake with them. Having tea with dragons? What more could she possibly hope for? Who knew that they even enjoyed tea? Granted, not every hostess served dried cod, roast whole pigeons, kippers, and small beer at tea, which made it all a little peculiar. But there were also some lovely little biscuits called madeleines, brought especially for her, that made her feel especially welcome. Even better, they were sweet enough to please April, who ventured out to sample them.

As they finished their tea, Castordale looked over his shoulder and beckoned someone toward them.

"Lizzy! I have been looking everywhere for you!" Uncle trundled up with a large parcel under one arm and an exasperated look on his face.

She swallowed back the lump in her throat. "This is where Rustle instructed me to wait. I have not moved from this spot, just as he told me."

Rustle landed on the back of her chair. "Indeed, she is where I instructed her to be. I do not know how you could have become confused."

"We have enjoyed her company greatly." Castordale smiled, at least insofar as a creature without lips could. "You need not worry. Please, Miss Elizabeth Bennet, consider yourself very welcome in our reading room the next time you come."

Elizabeth gasped and looked at Rustle, who glanced away and shook his head.

"Come now, Lizzy. It is late, and we need to return to Cheapside. I thank you all for keeping my niece company." He bowed from his shoulders and took Elizabeth's hand.

The walk home was a quiet one. Though she could feel no anger from Uncle Gardiner, there was a sort of heaviness—concern perhaps—that radiated from him. Perhaps she should not have talked to Storm, the drake who had approached her. But that would have been rude and ill-mannered. Truly, what was she supposed to have done? If only she could ask.

But conversation did not seem welcome at the moment. Perhaps at another time.

In the meantime, it would be difficult to keep the most remarkable day she had just spent all to herself. At least she would be able to record it all in her commonplace book.

10
Chapter

The next morning, after a breakfast that involved a great number of woeful remarks on Mama's part, Uncle Gardiner invited Elizabeth and April to come to his study. One might have thought he simply invented the need to talk to her in order to escape the morning room, but such subterfuge was unlike Uncle Gardiner. He must have some desire for conversation with her, however small—perhaps just to ask after April and how she enjoyed her morning jam.

Once inside the tidy, sunlit room that faced the street, he led her to a plain, narrow door opposite the window, beside his tall, uncluttered bookcase. He was obviously a well-read man, but managed to keep all his books in order and on the shelves. Perhaps, when one had as many books as Papa, the task became quite impossible. Tucked between the bookcase and corner, with a coat-tree in front of it, the unassuming entrance would have been very easy to miss.

"I thought you might be interested to see this." He pulled the coat-tree aside and opened the door to a very tiny, very plain room, with a single window, partially open.

The walls were plain boards, painted pale grey, as were the floor boards. A carved wooden perch stood in the center of the room, a few feather-scales on the floor beneath it. Though not nearly as ornate, it resembled the dragon perch kept in Papa's study. A small table held an empty tin plate with a few drops of gravy left at the very edge and a bowl of small beer, half drunk. Below the table sat the package Uncle had brought home yesterday from the Blue Order.

"This is a room dedicated to Rustle's use. Well, in all rights, it is more of a closet, but it is his nonetheless. This house has been home to many non-dragon hearing family members. It has served very well for him to have his own space where he might come and go as he likes. Though your mother grew up here, I am not certain she even knows about this space."

April launched from her shoulder and buzzed around the room, checking out the cobwebs in the high corners. Was she looking for insects to eat? She had never shown any preference for them before.

"It is a lovely idea that he should have a place of his own. Is he able to open the window himself?"

"A builder affiliated with the Order crafted the window to swing open like a French door, making it easy for him to operate. It is a feature incorporated into many dragon-friendly homes." He winked as he sidled past her to retrieve the package. He pushed aside the plate and set the curious object on the table, untying the strings that held the wrapping. "I think you both shall find this very dragon-friendly as well. I had intended to bring it to Longbourn as soon as it was ready, but it seems you have come for it yourself." He pushed away the brown paper to reveal a heavy quilted cover, like a tea cozy over the still mysterious domed object. "Pray, April come down and see. Go ahead, Lizzy, uncover it."

She unbuttoned the quilted wrapper, revealing white wrought-iron filigree shaped into a tall dome. "A cage?"

April squawked and flapped. "No, no, I will have no part of any cage."

"Let me show you. It is not a cage, although your mama and sisters will be persuaded, for everyone's good, that it is." He opened the little door and pointed at the lock. "Look closely. The lock is on the inside and can only be operated by a fairy dragon's beak—see how tiny the locking mechanism is. No one can lock you in, but you may lock others out."

April hopped toward it and pecked at the latch. It clicked, sliding out a bolt that would fasten the door in place. She pecked again, and it released. Cocking her head, she hopped to the other side. No, there was no such mechanism on the outside.

"How clever! You can come and go freely, but no one would suspect! That is brilliant and certainly not a cage." Elizabeth tested the door herself. The ironwork proved not only very sturdy, but very fine, with no rough edges to catch tender skin.

"There is more. See how the base is very thick? There is a reason." Uncle turned the cage slightly and revealed a sliding panel in the base. "Fairy dragons hate the cold. So you can slide a warm brick here, then cover the cage with the cozy to make it very warm inside, much like you might warm your bed before tucking in for the night."

Apparently dragons were not the only ones who could be persuasive.

April twittered happily. "A warm place for me?" She hopped inside. "Oh, a nesting box, and it is full of soft!"

Elizabeth giggled as April fluffed the bits of cotton wool and feathers inside the box.

"And a perch! Oh, up there—does that swing?" April flitted to the top of the cage where a dainty white swing hung down from the dome's apex.

Who would have known she would so enjoy flapping her wings and swinging?

"Oh! Oh! Is that a bath?" April dove toward a china bowl held in an iron scrollwork frame.

"Indeed, it is. I did not know whether you preferred water or dust, so it has not been set up yet, but let me know your preferences, and I will prepare it for you. Likewise, these dishes are for your victuals. These perches," he pointed to several small shelves affixed at various heights within the cage, "should permit you an excellent vantage point for anything you wish to observe from within. And—this is very special for the seamstress has only just worked out this design," he wrapped the cozy around the cage, adjusting it with the drawstring, "the cozy is crafted so that you may adjust it from inside, closing it if you want privacy or warmth, and opening it otherwise."

"I am astonished that anyone would have put so much thought and care into something designed for fairy dragons." Elizabeth ran her fingers along the top edge of the pale blue cozy.

"They are very dear little friends. Not everyone is

so impatient with them as is your father. There are a fair number in the Order who are very vocal in their support of them. I am glad you like April's new room. I hope you both shall enjoy it very much."

Elizabeth bit her knuckle. "I do not know that Papa will allow us to accept such an extravagant gift. I am quite certain it is not something he can afford."

Uncle dropped down to one knee beside her. "Oh, Lizzy. I know your father has been very difficult recently. It is complicated and difficult to understand, but pray, try to be patient with him. He is not a bad man—"

"Mr. Gardiner! Mr. Gardiner!" The housekeeper banged at the study door.

"Pray excuse me a moment." Uncle pulled the door closed behind him. Perhaps the housekeeper was persuaded not to be aware of this room so that Rustle might have his privacy.

The hinges on the study door complained as it swung open.

"Sir, pray. Mr. Bennet has come. What am I to do with him?"

"Gardiner!" Papa boomed. "I must speak with you immediately."

"Good morning, Thomas. Let us go to the parlor—"

"No. I must speak to you privately, before I address Fanny." Shuffling feet, and the door shut hard.

Elizabeth dropped down, tailor-style, on the floor and scooted into the far corner of the room. Papa should have no reason to come into Rustle's apartment, but if he did, it would not do for it to appear she was trying to listen in on their conversation.

Not that she had to try. Was it her superior hearing,

or were they really being that loud? Perhaps she could try to climb out of the window and make her way back in through the kitchen. But no, the window was too high to climb out of unless she had something to stand on, and moving the table would make too much noise. She was trapped for the duration.

"I know Fanny brought the girls here to stay with you."

"I have made no effort to keep that a secret from you. But I must be honest. Some of the things she has said this time sound concerning."

This time? Had Mama fled Longbourn before? Elizabeth closed her eyes. There were two occasions when Hill said Mama was in her rooms, unwell and not to be disturbed, but no sound ever came from Mama's rooms. It was not possible for Mama to be that quiet for that long. Perhaps she had been in London those times?

"What calumny is she speaking against me this time?"

Uncle harrumphed as though he meant to remark on Papa's words, then thought better of it. "Her complaints are much as they ever have been: that you refuse to take proper care of her and your daughters."

The sound of flesh on flesh—Papa must have slapped his forehead.

A slight breeze blew through the window, causing the feather-scales on the floor to flutter about. How pretty and soft they looked. Would Rustle mind if she took a few so she could draw them in her commonplace book? She would return them when she was done.

"You know that is complete nonsense. She and the girls are very comfortable. Truly, they want for—or perhaps more rightly I should say they are in need of—nothing."

"Fanny says that you do not intend to allow Jane to come out into society." Uncle rapped his knuckles softly, probably on his desk. He often did that when he talked.

Papa made that strangled sound in his throat that often came out when he and Mama argued. "That is hardly what I have said. How like her to misconstrue my intentions once again."

"Perhaps then it is time that I heard your side of the story."

"Fanny wants Jane to come out next year, at just fifteen. I think it foolhardy and far too young for coming out." Papa huffed and snorted, most likely he was wrapping his arms over his chest, too.

"It is not unheard of."

"But it is not sensible. Consider, your betrothed is nineteen, nearly twenty now, out only a year and about to be very well-settled. She is a practical, level-headed young woman, made so by the extra years she spent out of society. Jane will benefit from the same."

"Fifteen is a mite early to be out. But Fanny does have a point. Five daughters are a great many to marry off. And with your estate entailed away, should anything happen to you –we both know the state of your health …"

Papa was probably glaring now. His health was always a sore point of discussion, no matter who mentioned it.

"Yes, yes, I am entirely aware of the precarious situation of my family. Thank you so much for reminding me. And thank you even more for echoing the lack of faith that my wife places in my ability to care for my family."

A chair scraped along the floorboards. Uncle was probably pushing back from his desk, maybe getting ready to pace the floor. "She told me of your plan to marry Lizzy to your heir, whatever his name is. While it is certainly a possibility to be entertained, I think it far from a reliable scheme by which to insure provision for your family."

"While it is certainly my favored approach and the one I will continue to advocate for, I am well aware of the many ways in which it may go awry. My health is uncertain, and if I am not there to promote the match—well, you know how young people can be, choosing to do whatever is in their own minds rather than looking to the good of others. So, I have something else in mind as well."

"And what might that be?"

"You know I am in consideration to be the Historian of the Order."

"I had heard something along those lines."

Elizabeth wrapped her arms tightly around her waist. If he was not named Historian, it would be her fault …

"Our late Scribe, Sir Justin, his situation was much like my own. His estate was entailed away, and his wife and daughters could not hear dragons. Upon his death, the Order assigned them a stipend and a guardian to watch over their affairs, from a distance. It is my hope and expectation that, if I am made Historian, they will do the same for my family as well."

"You cannot be certain they will do that, though. He served the order for twenty-five years! His circumstances are so different—"

"He also petitioned for those provisions when he became Scribe. I will do the same, if I am made Historian. 'If' being the current operative word. I was so close to having sufficient votes to secure the post, then this affair with Lizzy! How she has complicated matters!"

"What are you talking about?" Uncle's chair creaked again.

"She is too young to be a Dragon Friend, yet that fool fairy dragon chose her. That event came to the attention of the Order. Now they insist she must be brought into full membership before I can be confirmed as Historian."

April snuffled softly, her feather-scales pouffing out as they did when she was upset. She paced along the edge of the table, softly chittering to herself. Good thing Papa was not in sight, or she would certainly have words for him now.

"That would explain why she was invited to the offices yesterday."

Feet landed hard on the floor. Papa was stomping again. "You brought her to the Order? How could you?"

"Rustle said her presence was required. What else could I do? She did nothing more than sit … in the parlor … and wait for me to pick up the fairy dragon cage."

"She was left alone in the offices?"

"Rustle was her chaperone."

"He did realize she was not to talk to unfamiliar dragons."

"I am assured that she behaved very well. She did you proud, Thomas. You have nothing to worry about from her." How neatly Uncle avoided mentioning that she had indeed done just what Papa feared she would.

But what choice did she have? She certainly could not have ignored Storm and his friends, much less Castordale. Rudeness to dragons was no less bad than rudeness to people.

"Nothing to worry about? Have you not been listening to anything I have said? Despite all my best efforts, it seems that all the plans for my family's future now ride on the shoulders of a very young and impetuous girl! You think that is nothing to worry about? If only she had not interfered with April, the vote would have happened as scheduled, and I would have been named as Historian at the next council meeting. Fanny and the girls would be secure, even if my heir does not marry Lizzy. But now? Anything can happen with that girl, and there is nothing I can do about it."

"You are worried for nothing. I am sure of it. I have every confidence in Lizzy."

"That is all well and good for you to say when you have no idea of how willful she can be."

Elizabeth swallowed hard. Was that what he thought of her?

"Willful is hardly a word I would use to describe her. You are seeing what you fear, not what is really there. Come, I am sure Fanny has been made aware of your arrival by now. You both need to talk. I am sure you can come to some agreement on Jane's coming out that will be acceptable to both of you."

Heavy foot falls, then the door opened and shut.

No wonder Papa had been so very hard on her. She had never meant to interfere with his plans, but it seemed she had. Now, somehow, she had to put that right. The only way to do that was to make sure she did not stand in the way of him being named Historian.

Whatever it took, she would prepare for and pass the Blue Order test and make him proud.

An hour later, Uncle Gardiner took Elizabeth and all her sisters to call upon Miss Wright, who would become Mrs. Gardiner when her father returned from the continent and they could be married. A bachelor going out with five little girls was quite an undertaking, especially walking the busy streets of London on a cloudy day that vaguely threatened rain. Uncle Gardiner proved surprisingly adept at managing Lydia, though, which was particularly fortunate when Lydia slipped from Jane's grasp and nearly ran into the street in front of a rapidly-driven coach. With a stern reprimand, he tucked Lydia under his arm and carried her the rest of the way, ignoring her loud protests. Eventually she cried, but when that did not soften his resolve, she quit the effort and quietly observed the scenery from her new vantage point. He would be a good father someday.

Miss Wright proved to be exactly the kind of woman it seemed Uncle Gardiner would be drawn to, pretty, practical, and very sympathetic. She shared an immediate connection with Elizabeth that went beyond words. It seemed destined that they should become very good friends in time. Her only real fault, it seemed, was that she did not hear dragons.

It was a wee bit troubling that Uncle Gardiner would marry a woman who did not hear. Had he not already seen what a trial it could be, having watched Mama and Papa? Or was it different for him since he was not a Keeper, but only a Friend? Certainly Rustle's needs were very different to Longbourn's. A minor dragon could live without a Friend quite comfortably and still maintain a good standing in the Order. Some minor dragons hatched wild—without the presence of humans to imprint upon—and had nothing to do with human society or the Blue Order. Major dragons and imprinted minor dragons kept them under close watch. Major dragons, though, had to have a Keeper. They required territory, and for that, men had to be involved.

Trying to manage the needs of a dragon estate, whilst keeping Mama ignorant of the true nature of things, had always proven difficult for Papa. True, Mama was a rather difficult sort of personality in her own right. But the unusual nature of her home only made it worse. Papa was an intelligent man. Could he not have foreseen how things could go so easily awry? Why would he have married Mama knowing that? Perhaps if it had been a love match, it might have made more sense—though it was difficult to imagine how a dragon-hearer might love someone who was not. Though her parents were fond of one another, it was hardly the stuff of love.

But maybe that was why Uncle Gardiner wanted to marry Miss Wright. If there had ever been a couple in love, no doubt, it was they. Even Rustle seemed to approve of her, and for such a crusty creature, that was saying a very great deal in her favor. And the way she looked at Rustle—it was peculiar, not the way Mama looked at Rustle or even April, but attentive, anticipatory even, as though Rustle might say or do something very interesting at any moment. There were times when it seemed Miss Wright might actually hear Rustle, just a bit, but then it seemed she did not. Such a quandary. At least she was very kind toward them all.

After they returned home, Mama's mood seemed

much improved, and Papa's, too. They announced that the family, with Uncle Gardiner's permission, would be staying in London for a fortnight to take in some of the sights and enjoy a change of venue. Something about the way Papa said it, though, did not ring entirely true.

The material thing was that Mama and Papa appeared to be at peace with one another, and that had to be a good thing. Even Rustle and April noticed the change as tensions in the house seemed to ease. That evening in the parlor, Uncle suggested a few outings that the family might find pleasing. Most remarkably, Papa agreed to consider several of the ideas. Perhaps a fortnight in London might prove fun after all.

Two days later, just after breakfast, the housekeeper burst into Jane and Elizabeth's room. "Miss Elizabeth, you are wanted in Mr. Gardiner's study immediately." The look on her face made it clear; this was no time for questions.

Elizabeth ran down the stairs behind the housekeeper, arriving breathless at the partially-open study door. She slipped inside and gasped. A very regal, very large jet-black cockatrice, wearing a satchel with a brooch bearing the Blue Order crest fastening the straps across his chest, perched on the back of a chair facing Uncle's desk. He was easily the most stunning minor dragon she had ever seen.

Uncle sat behind his modest desk, and Papa sat next to the cockatrice, their full attention on the stately creature. Papa slowly turned to look at her.

Gracious, what had she done? He was already so angry.

Uncle's expression was little better. "Lizzy, this is Turner, official messenger of the Blue Order." He gestured toward the cockatrice.

She reached for the edges of her cloak, but she was not wearing it. So, she curtsied deeply, bowing her head as far as she could. "I am honored to make your acquaintance."

Turner squawked an acknowledgement, his voice as proud and elegant as himself, and cocked his head at Papa.

He cleared his throat, running his finger around the edge of his cravat. "It seems the Order has decided that since we are already in London, it would be expeditious to conduct your admissions testing immediately."

She grabbed for the arm of the nearest chair, her face growing cold and prickly. "Immediately?"

"Immediately." Turner echoed, putting an end to all discussion with a decisive wing flap.

"But, pray, I am not ready. I am sure I am not. We were supposed to have six months to prepare." She tried to catch Turner's eyes, but he turned aside.

"You will present yourself at the Order offices in two hours for the examination." Turner squawked again and dove out the window before any further discussion could be raised.

Papa scowled at her. If only she could swoop out the window after Turner and disappear into the London skies herself.

Uncle leaned back into his chair behind his desk. "Do not blame her, Thomas. I assure you, Lizzy has done nothing to cause this."

"No, this is her mother's doing." Papa snarled, staring at the closed door as if Mama might be listening behind it. "If she had not brought the girls to London—"

"Perhaps that is so, but it matters very little whose

fault it is. What is done is done."

"But she is hardly ready." Papa bounced his fist against the upholstered chair arm. "We have barely finished working on the bestiaries. She does not know the histories, or all the treaty provisions, or—"

He was right. She choked back a sob. But it was not because she had been lax in her studies. There was just so very much to be learnt. Even six more months might not be sufficient.

How was it possible the Miss Delveses learned the same material she was being required to? It seemed as if they knew nothing at all. Surely they had been held to a different standard, but why? Was it Pembroke's rank that made it easier for them, or Papa's aspiration to be an officer that made it more difficult for her?

Uncle huffed a heavy breath. "There is no point in dwelling upon what she does not know. They are well aware they have only given you one-third of the allotted preparation time. I am sure that will be taken into consideration—"

"Then you hardly know the Blue Order. I would not be surprised if this were not some intentional ploy—"

"Enough! There is no need to concern Lizzy with the politics and personalities of the Order. The poor girl has enough on her mind." Uncle walked around the desk toward her.

She pressed her face into her shoulder, nodding.

"Calm yourself, my dear. I am sure you will do very well. I have it on good authority that there will be at least one dragon on the testing committee. We both know dragons have always been very sympathetic toward you. I am sure that will be strongly in your favor." Uncle smiled in what should have been an encouraging manner, but it felt forced. "Quickly, go upstairs and put on a clean frock. I will send the housekeeper to help you with your hair. We will leave in half an hour. Oh, and bring April as well. Turner said she was to attend with you."

Papa stomped and stood. "No, I absolutely draw the line at that. The fairy dragon is hardly more than a hatchling and knows nothing about proper behavior. She cannot possibly show herself to good report!"

Uncle snatched a paper off the desk and waved it in front of Papa. "You see the summons as clearly as I do. They require her presence as well. We have no choice."

Papa muttered again. Elizabeth dashed from the room, heart pounding so loud she could hardly breathe.

Half an hour later, she met Papa and Uncle Gardiner in the front hall. Her hands shook and her legs trembled so hard she could barely walk. April hid herself in the hood of her cloak, shivering so hard she hummed. Elizabeth had never heard her make that sound before. Poor little thing was even more afraid than she was. Perhaps the only thing keeping April from hysterical fits were Rustle's whispered assurances that the Order had never insisted upon the separation of Dragon Friends. That was some hope to hold onto.

Somehow, it seemed like the morning air should be more, well, distinct, on a morning such as this one. The sky should be heavy with clouds; the wind should be cold and sharp; the sun should not deign to show its face, hiding behind buildings and clouds. But alas, none of those forces seemed to pay attention to her distress. Callous and cruel, they ignored her and went about their way, creating a wholly unremarkable, reasonably pleasant morning.

Uncle held her hand as they walked to the Blue Order Offices. Papa's joints pained him a great deal today, so much so he could barely hold his own hat to put it on. Would he have held her hand if he could? Probably not a good thought to dwell upon right now.

The Order's doorman let them in and instructed them on where to await their escort; his tone was very grave and somber. Elizabeth gulped. Might this be the last time she would be privileged to enter this amazing place? A blue-liveried footman came for them and led them toward the back of the building, to a large but plain stone staircase lit by not quite enough candles, and down a long flight of stairs. They turned down a broad corridor with a polished limestone floor—sized for dragons and humans to pass—and strode to the end of the hall where a large oak door carved with vines and forest wyrms bore a painted plaque declaring *Undersecretary of the Blue Order—the Honorable Swinton St. John.*

Heavens, that was a rather presumptuous-sounding name. Under less serious circumstances, she and April would have laughed about it, taking turns imagining how the man behind the door might look. But today, laughter seemed very, very far away.

The footman pushed open the door, announcing their arrival. They stepped into a very large room, lined with narrow, high windows which would probably be near the level of the street outside. Mirrors reflected and magnified the light within the room, making it seem as if the windows were far larger than they were. Even with that, the room still felt dim, a little dingy and ominous.

A single large desk with several wingchairs surrounding it stood in the center of the room. Behind them, a large open doorway revealed a rough, rock passageway that disappeared into darkness. Uncle had told her there were many tunnels especially for dragons to use. That must be one of them.

The Honorable Swinton St. John stood behind his desk. He was a very average man, not what one might think of as "honorable." His hairline was receding, his belly paunchy, and his eyes close-set and squinty. His face was screwed up like he had a bad smell under his nose. That set him apart for distinction. Beside him, a brown drake the size of a pony, with a pointy spinal ridge trailing down his back, stood shifting his weight from one foot to the other. A faint, rotten odor permeated the room, rather like a smell she had noted in the barn once when the groom told her there was a horse with hoof rot. Were dragons subject to the same sort of malady? Perhaps that was why he seemed so very restless.

"My Friend, Rottenstone." Mr. St. John pointed to the drake as he looked at her with narrow eyes. "Is this the girl?"

What kind of an introduction was that for a Dragon Friend? How rude!

"This is my daughter, Elizabeth." Papa touched her shoulder.

She curtsied more from reflex than anything else.

"Leave her. I will send for you when we have determined her fitness to be part of the Order."

"I would rather stay." It seemed Papa was trying to sound forceful, but it did not quite happen.

"No. The rest of the testing committee has determined your presence could give the girl an unfair advantage. She will stand alone as every other prospective member of the Order does."

"Who is on the committee?"

"They have chosen to remain anonymous to you. Now go." Mr. St. John pointed.

The footman stood beside Papa, gesturing toward the door. He and Uncle left, the door echoing as it shut behind them.

Four somber figures walked in, each wearing the same blue robes with the Order insignia. They blended together, difficult to tell one from another—that was probably intentional—three men and one woman. Four large minor dragons followed them, two drakes, a wyrm, and—gracious! That was Castordale! She probably should not demonstrate her recognition, but it was a relief to see a familiar face.

"You have brought your friend, April?" Mr. St. John rapped the desk with his knuckles.

April crept out from her hood. "I am here."

"Proper behavior is expected at all times. Is that understood? There is to be no whispering, no singing, no signaling, no assistance given in any way, or you will be removed from the room." His voice boomed and echoed through the chamber. Did he really have to snarl at her? It was not as if April had done anything wrong.

April cheeped and huddled close to Elizabeth's neck. She cupped her hand over April until she stopped trembling.

"The panel will ask you questions. You will answer them, but make no other conversation. Do you understand?" Mr. St. John leaned forward on his elbows, making his glare just a little more threatening.

"May I ask for clarification if I do not understand a question?"

Mr. St. John glanced at the panel. They whispered among themselves for a moment. The tallest man looked at her. "You may ask for clarification, but we will determine if it is a valid question. If we consider it stalling or looking for a hint, you will be penalized. Understood?"

"Yes, sir." She clasped her hands tightly behind her back.

"The panel will continue until they are confident of their decision. Their determination will be final."

She nodded.

"Panel, you may begin." Mr. St. John gestured toward the committee, his voice echoing in the stark chamber.

Elizabeth gulped and licked her lips.

The first questions were simple, a recitation of the preamble of the Pendragon Accords, a brief statement of the history and the philosophy of the treaty and the land settlements that went with it. She had penned those in her commonplace book, one of the first dragon entries she had written there.

It was difficult to tell how the panel received her answers. They moved on to the next question without comment, or even a change in their shadowy expressions hidden by their hoods.

They continued quizzing her on the Pendragon Treaty for some time. The questions became more detailed, and for that, more difficult, coming in rapid fire, one after another. But it was material she knew well and felt certain of, so she breathed a little easier.

By the time they moved on to the major genealogies of English dragons, her shoulders ached, and she shifted from one foot to the other to ease the strain in her knees. The family lines of the firedrakes she knew well enough, but the amphitheres and the basilisks she stumbled on. How much would those mistakes count against her?

A bright, quivering drop of spittle gathered at the edge of Rottenstone's mouth—rather like a predator identifying easy prey. Rumblkins and the barn wyrms did that when they spotted a mouse or a rat. It was not a comforting expression. Rottenstone began a rapid-fire series of questions related to the dragon bestiaries. The first several she answered easily enough.

"Describe a basilisk."

"Greystoke's description or Blair's?" She asked, holding her breath. She knew Blair's better, it was more accurate—

"Edmonton's."

Her knees quivered a mite as she stammered and stuttered. "I … I have not read …"

"That is hardly our problem. Do you know the description of a basilisk or not?" Rottenstone stepped half a step closer, extending his head the way drakes did when they were trying to appear large and make an important point.

"I do sir, but from experience … not from a book."

"You have met a basilisk?" the woman gasped.

Elizabeth nodded vigorously. "Pembroke. He introduced himself to me whilst—"

"Liar. Presumptuous little liar. Basilisks are not social creatures and do not ever introduce themselves to casual acquaintances." She flicked her hand at Elizabeth.

"We were lost in his territory—"

"You were trespassing in a dragon's Keep?" one of the men snapped.

If only they would listen! "Not trespassing. The daughters of the Keep had taken me into the woods and we—"

"A place you had no business!"

April launched from Elizabeth's shoulder and buzzed toward the panel, growling under her breath. Fairy dragons were more funny than fierce when they growled. "You do not know what happened or what you are even talking about. They were horrid creatures, abusing my Elizabeth so that she became lost. They intentionally tried to—"

"Silence! No one is interested in what you have to say, fairy dragon." One of the drakes extended her frill and snarled at April.

"You cannot speak that way to her! She is every bit as much a dragon as the rest of you and is deserving of the appropriate respect!" Elizabeth stomped toward the panel.

The largest drake flared his hood and hissed at her. She spread her cloak and hissed back, stomping to mimic the sound of a slapping tail. Longbourn probably should not have taught her that trick.

The drake hopped a step back. The wyrm slid in front of him and puffed his body, weaving back and forth hypnotically in front of her.

She flipped her hood on, spread to its fullest and matched his movements, hissing and spitting with him. No, spitting was not ladylike, but it was dragon-like.

The smaller drake interposed herself between them. "Stop this unseemly behavior. This territory belongs to neither of you. Castordale is dominant here, not either of you."

All eyes turned to Castordale who rose up very tall and looked from the wyrm to Elizabeth.

At first his expression was severe, but then it softened. He met her gaze and began to laugh. Granted, it was a hiccoughy, hissing sort of sound, but it was definitely laughter.

He was laughing at her! She had made such a cake of things that all he could do was laugh!

She had failed not just Papa and Uncle Gardiner, but her entire family. Now their futures would be in jeopardy, all because she could not control her tongue and her temper.

She whirled on her heel, cape flying behind, and pelted out of the door, April barely able to keep up.

11
Chapter

She burst into the corridor and continued her blind run. Granted, she had no idea where she was going, but she should get there rather quickly. If only she could make her way to a staircase, she could probably find her way to the reading room where she had been welcomed before. Yes, that would be a reasonable place to go.

But Papa would eventually find her, and she would have to answer for her actions. He would, no doubt, lose his chance to become Historian, and she—the Blue Order would not deign to send her to any sort of school after this outburst. What would they do with her? Would they insist April leave her and find a new Friend?

Oh, it was all far too much! Her shoulders trembled, and her knees shook.

She paused a moment, clenching her fists and sucking in deep breaths. This was neither the time nor the place for tears. Dragons were far too practical for such theatrics. She must bring herself under better regulation.

"Stop! Wait!" That was a dragon voice. The sounds of a great number of men marching followed.

She swallowed hard and straightened her spine, pulling her shoulders back. The least she could do was make herself as big as possible for the encounter.

"Why did you run off?" Castordale stopped in front of her, blocking any chance of escape. They might not look like it, but snake-types were notoriously fast, especially on smooth ground like the limestone tiles of the hall.

She looked past him, at a spot at the end of the corridor, one that in normal buildings would have held a window, but in this one, sported a niche with a carved marble bust of a firedrake, a founder of the Order.

"No one threatened you. Why did you run?"

"What point was there to stay? Clearly I failed. I did not need to stay to be a laughingstock as well."

Castordale's forehead creased into funny little lines that folded his scales awkwardly. Was that uncomfortable? "Laughingstock? I have no idea what you mean."

She looked straight into his eyes and rose on tiptoes. "You were laughing at me."

The corner of his mouth turned up a bit. "True enough. I was."

"I think it awfully rude of you to do so. It is enough that I could not answer the question put to me. Why could you not leave it at that? Laughing at me over it was just cruel." April pressed tight against the side of her neck. She was probably trying to be comforting, but her feather scales tickled.

His bobbed his head from side to side, deep blue

scales glinting in the candlelight. "I suppose that is one way to see it. I have little experience with young ladies. My Keeper has only sons, as did my prior two Keepers. It seems you are a different creature to the young men I have known." His long, green tongue tasted the air near her.

"I do not think that is a compliment."

"There are sufficient individuals who consider women silly and flighty and insufficient to the task of dragon-keeping in general that I can see why you would think that."

"Do not insult my Elizabeth!" April hovered near Castordale's nose. Her tiny blue form blended into Castordale's blue scales, making her a little hard to follow. "She is the best Friend a dragon could have. Ask Longbourn. She is an excellent Keeper even now. Why do you horrid creatures seem utterly determined to keep her away from her natural place?" She landed on Castordale's nose and pecked it sharply.

He blinked, more surprised than injured. No doubt his hide was thicker than human skin. "Natural place? Now that is an interesting thought—one that I would like to further explore. Come with me. I shall send for some tea, and we shall have a bit of a chat." Castordale slithered past her, beckoning her with the tip of his tail.

What else was she to do? She followed him.

They traveled down a staircase—it was interesting to watch him slither down two levels—such intricate movements it entailed—through several long, dimly-lit corridors, and through a large door made to open by pulling a heavy cord. Castordale could not have easily managed a doorknob.

Candles in wall sconces, few and far between, lit the rough passage behind the door. It was not really rough so much as it was unfinished. The walls and floor were smoothly-hewn rock, but without floor boards, tile, or plaster, they felt unrefined, rather like the cellar at Longbourn. But, after a fashion, they were also snug and cozy, a little familiar-feeling.

How Mama and her sisters would raise their eyebrows to hear her call such a place snug and even comfortable. But it was. The glow of the candles was warm and inviting, a friendly flickering in glowing tones. Without decoration, the surroundings did not distract from her company, leaving her free to consider whom she was with and why she might be there. If anything, it made his company seem even more important.

It might have been frightening, if one did not trust dragons. But the Pendragon Treaty made it clear that Castordale would not harm her. The repercussions of such an act were too great. In fact, the treaty ensured that major dragons would almost always be more constrained in their behavior than most people.

There was a reason she tended to prefer dragon company.

The tunnel split, and they took the right fork, which soon widened into a large, comfortable room, lit with an arrangement of candles and mirrors in each corner. Along one side, there was a carved hollow lined with soft hay—and was that down? Castordale was clearly a fellow who liked his comfort. A shelf along an adjacent wall held a number of scrolls, one partially unrolled along the top. It seemed he also read, maybe extensively. When one lacked hands and feet, scrolls might just be easier to manage than books. That was something for her commonplace book. Hmmm, how might books be made more manageable for a snake-type dragon?

"You look very thoughtful, Miss Elizabeth Bennet." Castordale nosed a stool upholstered with thick leather padding toward her.

"Forgive me, sir." She curtsied. "I was just noticing your scrolls and thinking how books might be made more easily read."

With the tip of his tail, he gestured for her to sit. The corner of his mouth lifted, and he shook his head, laughing again.

She sat down and wrapped her arms around her waist. She probably should not frown so, but really, was it reasonable to assume she would not when she was constantly being laughed at?

"Forgive me. I forgot you do not like to be laughed at. But really, laughter is not such a bad thing. Is it not an expression of pleasure among warm-bloods?" Castordale curled comfortably in his soft hollow.

"It can be, but that is not always the case. Laughing with someone is often a good thing, a bit of fellow-feeling that bonds a relationship. But being laughed at, well, it is different."

"Indeed, how so? I have never had it explained to me." He cocked his head and lifted an eye ridge in a genuinely inquisitive expression.

"It is a means of belittling someone, telling them that they have done something very wrong, very silly, or stupid. I think it is a way of suggesting they are not ... not ... " Her voice broke. Gracious, how often had Mama laughed at her for her oddities—generally dragon-related. "That they are neither good enough, nor likely to ever be so. That they are trivial and worthy to overlook." She dragged her sleeve over her eyes. He had asked for an explanation. It might not be a very good one, but now he had it.

"Goodness!" Castordale sat back on his coils. "Why has no one ever explained this before? It is quite astonishing to know the expression seems to mean two very different things."

"Have you ever asked before?"

"I suppose not."

"I suppose you have also not had a young woman to ask. People rarely laugh at young men, at least in my experience."

"Another interesting observation. I will pay attention and see if that is a general experience."

A pair of small drakes with livery badges around their necks scurried in, bearing a tray with a tea service and a large tankard of something rather pungent.

"I blend my own tea and prefer it in amounts more appropriate to my size than those tiny cups you use." He chuckled and nosed the tankard a little closer to her.

She leaned over and smelt it. A very great deal of mint and other things she did not quite recognize. "April is rather fond of chamomile tea, especially with honey in it, though it makes her very sleepy."

Castordale looked at April. "You persuaded her to give you tea?"

"No, I simply asked." April shrugged and perched near the jam pot.

Castordale flicked the lid off the pot with his tongue. "Please, enjoy. I did not know whether you would prefer biscuits or sandwiches with your tea, Miss Elizabeth Bennet, so please, help yourself. I do not stand on a great deal of ceremony."

Elizabeth poured a cup of tea and sipped it quietly.

"You seem thoughtful again."

She set her tea cup down. "Forgive me. I was merely considering what you said: that you do not stand on a great deal of ceremony."

"You think I have lied?"

"No, not at all. It just seems that perhaps it is a different form of ceremony that you favor. Dragon introductions and greetings have a great deal of ceremony to them. At least, so it seems to me."

Castordale lifted his tankard with his jaws and somehow managed to take a sip of tea without spilling it. The cup must have been especially designed for the purpose. A normal cup would have tea running down his face and neck. "I suppose you could consider that a form of ceremony, if you look at it in a warm-blooded sort of way. But really, it is not. It is about—"

"Establishing dominance and precedence. I know, but is that not what most human ceremony is about?"

This time he threw back his head and laughed a deep, full-bellied rumble. "So it is, Miss Elizabeth Bennet. So it is."

"Why are you laughing at me?" She shook her fists at her sides.

"I am not laughing at you. Truly I am not. I am laughing at others who are not here."

"Pray forgive me. I do not follow."

"Ah, dear girl, I am sure there is a great deal you do not follow." He shifted into a position which resembled nothing so much as a large man settled comfortably into his favorite chair. "You and your little friend," he flicked his tongue at April whose head was still in the jam pot, "have caused rather a stir among the Order. I might add, it is not a bad thing. Sometimes things need to be shaken up a bit when they have gone old and stale."

"Papa does not approve of things being shaken, as you call it."

"I am not surprised. However, his opinion is not the only one, thankfully. There are those who wonder how a girl of just over a decade can possibly be trusted with the weight of the truth about dragons."

"Papa has made me very aware of that." She wrapped her arms around her waist and crumpled in on herself just a little. Appalling posture, Mama would call it, but clearly Castordale did not care about such things.

"I can imagine. Forgive me, but he has all the subtlety of a basilisk."

She sniggered under her breath. "From Greystoke's, Blair's, or Edmonton's bestiary?"

Castordale's expression shifted into something very serious, even troubled.

She bit her lip and winced. Perhaps that was not an appropriate jest.

"There is no Edmonton's Bestiary."

She blinked several times. "Excuse me? That cannot be possible. Was I not asked specifically—"

"Yes, you were, but there is no such book."

"But why then? I do not understand."

"Of course, you do not. You have not been alive long enough to understand the wiles of living in a world such as ours." He took another long sip of his tea, slurping just a bit. How did one make that sound without lips?

"I may not understand very much, but I would like to understand this."

"We live in a very precarious balance, dragons and men. Those who cannot hear dragon voices look upon us with fear and loathing. We must protect ourselves from them. The Blue Order exists to give us a way to do so while sustaining a mutually-beneficial peace with the warm-bloods and other dragons with whom we must share this world. But even within the Order, there have been those who sought to take advantage of dragonkind, who were not committed to maintaining the Pendragon Accords."

"Have there not been dragons with the same problems, though?"

"Indeed, there have." Now it was Castordale's turn to seem thoughtful. "But it seems we have a better record in managing those individuals than humans do."

She winced. "You mean you do not hesitate to send a larger dragon to dispatch them quickly."

"A crude way of putting it, but essentially true. It is difficult for men to grasp the nature of solitary creatures with predator-prey relationships."

"I suppose so. But do not drakes often form communities? That is what the book I found in the reading room said."

Castordale laughed again, so it was probably best she just resign herself to it at this point. "I knew you were going to say that. The rest of the group assured me I was wrong, but I knew you would say that."

"Excuse me?"

"Had our conversation in St. John's office continued, someone would have brought up the matter to see how you responded."

She pressed her temples hard. "You mean they would have picked an argument with me over the matter, rather like over the characteristics of a basilisk?"

"Exactly like that."

"But why? It does not make any sense. It even seems rather cruel."

"On that point, I will have to disagree." He downed another gulp of his tea. "When you consider the grave importance of the sort of decision we have been asked to make, I am quite comfortable that our tactics have been entirely appropriate."

"How is my admission to the Order that important?"

"Every member presents another potential source of danger to dragonkind, so they must be considered carefully, especially one as unusual as you. Doubly so when that one is in line to be a Keeper."

"Me, a Keeper? You jest. Women are not Keepers. We may be given the title as a courtesy, sometimes, but I hardly think it has any substance to it."

"Longbourn has asked for you."

"He is a very dear creature, though I am not even supposed to know him yet." If only he were here, he could take her through the fabled dragon tunnels back home and let her be done with this awful chapter.

"He had told us so, and a great many other things, including how he believes you are a very fitting member for the Order."

She swallowed past the aching lump in her throat. "I am sure he will be most disappointed to learn I have failed."

Castordale leaned back and cocked his head, studying her. "What do you think you were to be tested on?"

"A great many things, according to Papa: the Pendragon Accords, the genealogies, the bestiaries—"

"You think that is the core of our concerns?"

"I thought it was … but now I do not know what to think."

"But I do." He pulled up straight, almost tall enough to brush the top of the chamber with his head.

She worried her hands together.

"I have never seen such a thing as what you did with that garment of yours. And spitting at the wyrm!"

"Pray do not remind me. It was horrid and unlady-like." She covered her face with her hands.

"And utterly spectacular! A truly splendid demonstration of greeting etiquette, the likes I have never seen before."

"What did you say?" She peeked through her fingers.

"We had heard your understanding was superb—a bit unrefined perhaps, but truly a cut above, and we were not disappointed."

"But my behavior was shocking."

"Only to warm-bloods, I am sure. We found it quite refreshing. And perhaps more important to you, quite acceptable."

"But the panel—"

"They will rail about it, to be sure. They always do. It is their way of trying to assert dominance. But I know that more than one agrees with us already. We will prevail—after all, we have teeth." He bared his fangs in rather a playful way. By Heavens! They were enormous!

Wait—what had he just said? "Acceptable?"

"It is clear that you think like a dragon—even though you may have a great deal to learn yet. And anyone who thinks like a dragon belongs in the Order."

Castordale escorted her upstairs to the reading room, still the comfortable, happy, welcoming place it had been days ago. Storm, Cloudy, Mist, and Thunder were only too happy to chaperone her and teach her to play their favorite card game, a variant of whist that was both delightfully complex and full of draconic nuances of dominance and territorial claims.

Many rubbers later, Rustle winged his way into the room. Storm invited him to play. Surprisingly, he did. Who would have thought Rustle could play cards, much less want to? Moreover, he proved quite adept, beating the drakes rather soundly.

At the end of the rubber, though, he said, "I was sent to escort you back to Cheapside."

"Without Papa or Uncle?" Longbourn estate was the only place she had ever walked alone.

"They are both needed in meetings at the moment. We may take the dragon tunnels all the way to your Uncle's warehouse. From there, I will persuade a shop assistant to walk you home. We will tell your mother that an unexpected shipment has arrived. Your father will be assisting Gardiner with it all night."

"The meetings are expected to go on that long?"

"Indeed, they are. It goes that way sometimes. There are those who like to be stubborn for the power that it gives them. Another form of dominance as it were." Rustle winked.

Dragons winked? It made sense that they could, but seemed a little surprising that they actually did.

Elizabeth nodded. There was little she could do and asking questions would be considered untoward—at least her father would say so. Dragons might feel differently, but after such an agreeable afternoon, it was not the sort of thing one wanted to take a chance on. And it meant she would have the opportunity to see the fabled tunnels that ran under the city. Certainly that was something to celebrate.

Rustle led her down a small staircase, one she would

have thought to be a servants' stair in a typical building, but the Blue Order Hall was anything but typical. Many, many steps followed before the staircase finally ended, but at last it did, in a narrow, dimly-lit corridor, near a plain door. The corridor extended a long way to the left, disappearing into the distance.

"That leads into the Great Courtroom. That is for another day. Come." Rustle flapped to the door and pulled the latch rope with his beak. Just inside the door, a barrel held unlit torches. "Take one and light it from the candles in the hall."

Elizabeth obeyed. The torch was heavier than she had expected, and burned a little hotter than candles did, releasing an odd, somewhat unpleasant smell as it burned, unlike anything she had smelt before.

"Quickly now. You must get back to Cheapside before sundown." Rustle beckoned.

The hewn stone walls of the tunnels were large enough to admit a firedrake, or at least she imagined they would, having never seen one herself—yet—she could not be certain, but it certainly seemed so. Several small dragons, or people, could walk abreast in the cool, dark expanse. The smooth walls and floor set the tunnels apart from a naturally-formed cave, but only a fool would believe that made them safer for one who became lost in them without light. Even without the hazards of steep drops and collapsing floors, the darkness would be very difficult for one who could not see in the dark to find their way out. Most dragons possessed other senses that enabled them to get around underground, or at least so she had read. Someday, it would be interesting to talk to one directly about it.

The tunnels twisted and turned, splitting off at multiple forks. Which signposts did Rustle use to navigate?

Obviously he knew where he was going, never hesitating to make a turn, but Elizabeth could not make out any markers which would allow an unfamiliar traveler to identify one turn from another. And he flew so fast! By the time he stopped at a small doorway, Elizabeth was panting hard and nearly out of breath.

The doorway—of course—led to a long, narrow, steep staircase that seemed like it might never end. At last it did, with a large barrel—probably for her torch—near a narrow door. Rustle pecked the door open. She extinguished the torch, and followed him out. They emerged in a dark cellar with large crates blocking their view. Skirting around them, she heard noises and voices above. They were underneath Uncle Gardiner's warehouse!

Though it was said that cockatrice were not as good at persuasion as other dragons, Rustle was quite effective in convincing one of the shop assistants of Uncle Gardiner's supposed whereabouts and of the message he was to bring—along with Elizabeth—to the house at Cheapside. Elizabeth and the dispatch were delivered to Uncle Gardiner's housekeeper in short order.

It was hardly surprising that Mama was unhappy with the news she would be deprived of adult company that evening, but with a few suggestions from April and Rustle, she decided that an evening spent playing parlor games with her daughters might not be such a bad thing after all.

The next morning, the housekeeper woke her with the news that she was wanted at Mr. Gardiner's warehouse immediately and that she would take Elizabeth there on her way to do the morning's marketing. Rustle met them just outside the kitchen and accompanied them to the warehouse where he managed the few necessary persuasions to allow Elizabeth into the cellar and thence to the stairs into the dragon tunnels.

It would have been nice if Rustle had permitted her to catch her breath a bit when they arrived at the offices, but he immediately insisted they trek up the long, long, staircase as soon as they arrived. How was she ever going to make it up the hundreds of stairs up? And why was everything so hurried? Unless they were hungry or threatened, dragons almost never rushed.

Happily, they stopped at a landing that must have been only two-thirds of the way up. She clutched the railing.

"Wait here. Do not go anywhere. I must announce your arrival." Rustle flapped away, up the stairs, disappearing around a corner.

He really need not have ordered her to stay, for her feet were so heavy that she could do little else but sink into the nearest hall chair and gulp in deep breaths of cool, slightly damp air.

Her heart had just slowed to a normal pace when Rustle landed on the oak railing nearest her. "The committee will see you now."

She was to face them again? It would have been kind to have warned her of what was about to happen, but that was not the way dragons tended to think. If one could not see what was coming up ahead, one probably deserved to be eaten, or at the very least surprised. Not the most appealing of dragon traits, but so it was.

Rustle led her up the remaining stairs to a room she had not seen before. He rapped at the broad oak door with his beak. Though finely-crafted, the door bore no carvings, no name plaque to announce what might lie behind. It swung open into a large, oval room, lined with candelabras and mirrors working hard to cast light into the dark chamber, but there was no discernable furniture within. What kind of a room was this?

She blinked several times as her eyes adjusted. The dragons from the committee, including Castordale, gathered in a loose group along one side of the room. Maybe four other dragons joined them, but it was difficult to tell for certain how many there were in the dim light. Across from them, no less than a dozen blue-robed figures milled about. Some seemed vaguely familiar—probably the committee who had bombarded her with questions the day before. The rest were totally unknown. Probably just as well, for they all seemed grumpy and irritable and would probably be most unpleasant. But why were there so many here?

"Miss Elizabeth Bennet," that was Mr. St. John's voice booming from the middle of the room.

"Yes, sir." She tried to hold her voice steady, but she may as well not have tried. Her tone was high and thin, anything but confident. Exactly the way one should not sound around dragons.

"Step forward." Mr. St. John gestured as the dragons gathered on one side and the blue-robed figures on the other, making a loose ring around him.

With an encouraging chirrup from Rustle, she pulled her shoulders back and stepped toward Mr. St. John. If she could show confidence she did not feel, it could only be a good thing. Or so Longbourn had told her.

Mr. St. John folded his arms and cleared his throat. "Despite debate which has extended all night, the committee remains undecided about what should be done with you, Miss Bennet. In cases such as these, it has always been the way of the Blue Order to err on the side of caution. Therefore, your petition will not be—"

A roar echoed from the large entryway at the back of the room. A very familiar roar.

She looked over her shoulder at Rustle.

He shrugged his wings and muttered something about not everyone who had a say in the matter had been given proper voice. He kept his face carefully turned away though, not quite disingenuous, but definitely suspicious.

The dragons in the room froze in their places while the Order Members turned toward the tunnel, jaws gaping. Castordale slithered toward the entry, tail tapping the stone floor. He was annoyed, but it was not entirely clear at whom.

Another roar, this time much louder, and much grumpier, and the heavy thumps of angry, hurried footfalls. Longbourn burst into the room, nearly running over Castordale who blocked the entry.

"You have not been invited to this meeting," Castordale declared rather mildly, given the circumstances.

Dragons never reacted to surprises well. Did Castordale have something to do with this?

"My Keep is involved. It is an insult that I have not been invited." Longbourn stomped and slapped his tail at the same time. He was very, very annoyed. What joy there would be now. Annoyed dragons were hardly sensible.

"The child is not your concern." Mr. St. John walked slowly, deliberately toward Longbourn.

"According to whom? She is my Keeper's and is the oldest child who hears. She is to be the next Keeper." Longbourn pulled up as tall as he could, towering above everyone in the room.

"She is a girl! Estates are inherited by men." Mr. St. John rolled his eyes.

"She can marry the heir and be my Keeper."

"The Blue Order no longer arranges the marriages of its Keepers."

"Since when?" Longbourn's tail swept the floor, forcing a number of blue-robed figures to dodge.

"It is changing now. All the more reason that you should not be here."

"That does not change her fitness for the Order, and that is why I am here." Longbourn bellowed, softly for him, but it still left her covering her ears and cringing.

"What makes you think she is a fit member?"

Longbourn sidled past Castordale and thumped into the center of the room where he nudged Elizabeth. She scratched behind his ears. "You know you should not be here. You should not get yourself into trouble over me."

"That is for me to decide, not you." He extended his wing and pulled her close.

He was cold and scaly and a little musty-smelling. For that reason alone, his embrace should not have been comforting, but the strength of his support and powerful presence around her left her feeling safe in the midst of what seemed hostile adversaries.

"I have known about her since the first time she spoke to Rustle when she was but four years old. He told me about her then, that she was unlike any human child he had ever known. What four year-old approaches a cockatrice for conversation?" He chuckled—how odd it sounded when he held her close to his chest. "So I watched her, and Rustle was entirely right. She is unlike any Dragon Mate I have ever known. My Keeper did not introduce her to me, so I introduced myself after she had saved a clutch of fairy dragon eggs from freezing over winter."

April twittered at him. He nodded at her with a companionable smile.

"Which of you met your first major dragon without fear, much less without a proper introduction? Turn away such a warm-blood from the Order now, and she very well might not have you when you see fit to properly welcome her." He slapped his tail for emphasis. "Your rejection will not keep her away from dragonkind."

A gasp—entirely human—circled the room.

"Refuse a welcome from the Order, after she has applied for it? That is unheard of!" Mr. St. John sputtered, red-faced.

Castordale slithered between Longbourn and Mr. St. John. "No, no, I think Longbourn is quite right. If, untutored, she can face a basilisk in his own territory, without hesitation—and I did interview Pembroke to verify those details—I can hardly see why she would find you very intimidating, sir."

Mr. St. John's mouth worked like a trout held out of water. Around him, whispers and snorts circled the room.

Elizabeth swallowed hard. A thousand words fought for voice, but somehow it did not seem wise to interfere in the affairs of these dragons, at least not yet. Longbourn waded into the fray, stomping into the midst of the loudest argument.

Rustle urged her back toward the far end of the room, offering her a chair and whispering, "They may be at this for some time."

He was right, but it was impossible to tell how much

time passed. With no clocks and no sunlight to mark the hours, only the rumble in her belly suggested it might be near dinner. Then again, it might not; she had not eaten much of a breakfast. Not that it mattered. No one was paying her any mind at all.

Finally someone, probably Mr. St. John, bellowed for order, but no one paid him any heed. Finally, he stomped to Elizabeth and handed her something small and heavy.

"With so little sleep and so many in high dudgeon, there will be no proprieties today. Take this and go home. Rustle will take you to your family."

"What is this?" She turned it over in her hand.

"It is your signet. It will admit you into any Order establishment. Use it to seal any correspondence with the Order."

"Does that mean—"

"Welcome to the Order, Miss Bennet." He bowed and returned to the hubbub in the center of the room.

The next day, Elizabeth stood in the study between Papa and Uncle Gardiner, who sat in front of the desk. Afternoon sun streamed through the window, making it just a bit too hot to be comfortable. April seemed to enjoy it a very great deal, though.

Papa turned her signet over clumsily in his hands, peering closely through his glasses. A braided blue cord looped through the short brass handle holding the carved oval signet. The speckled green stone—dragon's blood jasper according to Storm—bore the engraved image of the Order's crest, a pair of dragons, tails entwined, holding a shield between them. Such a beautiful, precious thing, it was difficult to hand over, even for a moment.

"It is authentic, there is no doubt of that." Papa frowned as though it were a bad thing. Why did he do that? "And you are certain? He just handed it to you, without further ceremony, and dismissed you from the office?"

She clasped her hands tightly behind her back. "Yes, sir. Mr. St. John seemed quite certain—tempers would take some time to soothe, and there was no point in me continuing to wait upon that to happen. He did mention something about it still being essential that I formally come out to the Order, but for now, April and I might go about our way."

Papa placed the signet back in her hands. "A Blue Order Cotillion is naught but a waste of time and money when it is already established—"

Uncle clapped his forehead. "Thomas, you know very well none of that has been established—a great many things can change between now and then. If the cotillion is their only additional requirement in accepting Elizabeth, then I think you should count yourself grateful that the matter is settled so easily. So much, is, in fact, settled to your satisfaction." He raised his eyebrow and shot Papa such a look.

Did that mean Papa had been accepted as Historian? She cocked her head at them both.

"She deserves to know." Uncle harrumphed.

Papa wrinkled his lips the way he did when he was considering something. "The vote has been taken. I received word this morning."

"You are now Historian of the Order?" She clasped her hands before her heart.

He nodded, a hint of a smile at the edges of his lips.

Elizabeth bounced on her toes, clapping softly. "I

am so happy for you, Papa!"

"Yes, yes, it remains to be seen how it all goes, but for now, I am much satisfied." He nodded, rocking forward slightly as he did.

Did that mean he had also negotiated a stipend for Mama in the case of his death? It was certainly not a question she could ask, not now, and perhaps not ever. But at least it was a possibility, and if it did not happen, it would not be her fault. She held her breath, lest she breathe a sigh of relief.

"Now, off with you, Lizzy, and do not let your mother see your signet lest she decide your sister needs such a bauble herself."

"Yes, sir." She curtsied and scurried off toward the door, a little relieved Papa did not have further questions about her audience with Mr. St. John. Something about the way he was handling everything suggested that he did not know all the details of how her testing went. Perhaps it was best that way.

She paused near the foot of the stairs. Mama's voice drifted down from above. She was telling someone, perhaps Jane, that Papa had promised to take her to the theater tonight and to some sort of a party afterwards.

A party? Papa? That was terribly odd. But then Mama mentioned something about a Mrs. St. John as well. Why would they invite Mama to a party?

Best not head upstairs now. If Mama saw her, she would surely have to listen to far too many effusions on the joys of being in town. Today was not the sort of day she could listen to such things with a sweet smile and much nodding and admiration. She ducked out of the back door, into the little garden in the mews.

Rustle squawked a greeting from the dust bath in

the center of the rose bushes. They were not blooming and would not for months yet, but the leaves did a nice job of obscuring the empty patch in the center of the garden. Mama knew about it, though, and it seemed no amount of Rustle's persuasion could dissuade her from insisting to Uncle Gardiner that a proper gardener needed to be hired to "fix" the garden. Uncle listened to her, always very patiently, but never acted upon her advice.

Elizabeth sat near the roses, upwind of Rustle's dust bath so she could avoid sharing his toilette. He was very energetic in kicking up the dirt.

"Do you want to ask to join him?" She scratched April under the chin.

April sneezed. "Not today. Dust makes my nose itch."

Rustle flapped over to them and perched on the far end of the bench. "It is nice to have matters settled now." He flipped his wings neatly to his back.

Mama would declare him a horrid, dirty creature, covered in dust and a few dried rose leaves and petals. But the dust would fall away soon, carrying with it many of those things which made dragons the itchiest creatures in the kingdom. They were funny that way— they could always be counted upon to enjoy a good scratch.

"It does seem that way." She chewed her lip.

"You do not seem very content." He cocked his head at her and scratched behind his ear. Though cockatrice were dignified creatures, there was nothing dignified about his current posture.

"Oh, they both seem very happy right now, Mama and Papa. Truly, I cannot be anything but glad for that." She sighed, pulled her knees under her chin and wrapped her arms around them. "But it is not something to become too comfortable with, I fear. It never seems to last very long. I cannot remember a time when they got along well more often than not. It makes me wonder why they ever married."

"Perhaps having a baby come along so very soon after their wedding taxed your mother's nerves?" Rustle blinked and shuffled his feet. He looked aside, as though he had said something he should not have.

"I suppose. Jane was so sickly, too, or so I am told. Perhaps that contributed. But somehow it seems all this would be far easier if Mama heard dragons and could share that with him." It was strange being able to say such things aloud. It was not the sort of thing one shared to general acquaintances.

"That is difficult, indeed." Rustle scratched at the bench.

"Miss Wright cannot hear dragons." Elizabeth chewed her knuckle. "Do you think that will make Uncle Gardiner unhappy? Why have you not warned him about it?"

"Do you not like Miss Wright?" He hopped closer.

"I like her a very great deal; that is the problem. I do not want to like her if she will make Uncle unhappy."

"I do not think she will."

"How do you know?"

"I am not exactly sure. You came to hear dragons very young, you know."

"You were the first dragon I ever spoke to." She reached for him, and he extended his neck so she could reach under his chin to scratch.

"And you were the first child I ever spoke to. But it did not surprise me. I could see that you were one who could hear."

"See? How?"

He shrugged. "I cannot say. I just knew."

"So you think Miss Wright can hear?" She addressed a particularly itchy spot between his wings, and he cooed.

"Not yet, but just between you and I, I firmly believe that she will."

"But she is too old for that, is she not?" She stopped scratching, but only for a moment. He twitched his wings in protest, and she returned to her ministrations.

"Some come into their hearing much later than others. It is as unusual as you coming in so early, but not unheard of."

"I am glad for them both then. Do you think there is any chance—"

"No, your mother will never hear dragons. But considering her nerves, it is probably for the best." He half-snorted a laugh.

"I suppose so. And my sisters? Do you think any but Mary might hear?"

"I should not tell you. It would be too tempting for you to push them into it before they are ready. That would only cause problems for all of you."

Elizabeth harrumphed. His reasoning was sound, but she did not have to like it. But at least, he did not say "no." That meant another one of her sisters might hear, too, and Elizabeth could offer her a proper introduction to dragons. How lovely that would be, having someone with whom to share her dragon adventures. Perhaps she might even travel with her and Papa. That would be truly lovely.

Pray that it might be Jane. It would be lovely if Jane heard dragons, too.

Want more books in the series?
Pemberley: Mr. Darcy's Dragon
Longbourn: Dragon Entail
Netherfield:Rogue Dragon
A Proper Introduction to Dragons
The Dragons of Kellynch
Kellynch:Dragon Persuasion
Dragons Beyond the Pale

For more dragon lore check out:
JaneAustensDragons.com

Acknowledgments

So many people have helped me along the journey taking this from an idea to a reality. Debbie, Anji, Julie, Ruth, and Raidon thank you so much for cold reading and being honest!
My dear friend Cathy, my biggest cheerleader, you have kept me from chickening out more than once! And my sweet sister Gerri who believed in even those first attempts that now live in the file drawer!
Thank you!

Other Books by Maria Grace

Darcy Family Christmas Series:
Darcy and Elizabeth: Christmas 1811
The Darcy's First Christmas
From Admiration to Love
Unexpected Gifts

Given Good Principles Series:
Darcy's Decision
The Future Mrs. Darcy
All the Appearance of Goodness
Twelfth Night at Longbourn

**Behind the Scene Anthologies
(with Austen Variations):**
Pride and Prejudice: Behind the Scenes
Persuasion: Behind the Scenes

Non-fiction Anthologies
Castles, Customs, and Kings Vol. 1
Castles, Customs, and Kings Vol. 2
Putting the Science in Fiction

Available in e-book, audiobook and paperback

Available in paperback, e-book, and audiobook format at
all online bookstores.

About the Author

Six-time BRAG Medallion Honoree, #1 Best-selling Historical Fantasy author Maria Grace has her PhD in Educational Psychology and is a 16-year veteran of the university classroom where she taught courses in human growth and development, learning, test development and counseling. None of which have anything to do with her undergraduate studies in economics/sociology/managerial studies/behavior sciences. She pretends to be a mild-mannered writer/cat-lady, but most of her vacations require helmets and waivers or historical costumes, usually not at the same time.

She writes Gaslamp fantasy, historical romance and non-fiction to help justify her research addiction.

She can be contacted at:

author.MariaGrace@gmail.com

Facebook:
http://facebook.com/AuthorMariaGrace

On Amazon.com:
http://amazon.com/author/mariagrace

Random Bits of Fascination (http://RandomBitsof-Fascination.com)

Austen Variations (http://AustenVariations.com)

White Soup Press (http://whitesouppress.com/)

On Twitter @WriteMariaGrace

On Pinterest: http://pinterest.com/mariagrace423/

CPSIA information can be obtained
at www.ICGtesting.com
Printed in the USA
LVHW030748220821
695831LV00003B/255

9 780998 093789